THE SECRET SIGN OF THE LIZARD PEOPLE

KEVIN E. BUCKLEY

 FriesenPress

Suite 300 - 990 Fort St
Victoria, BC, V8V 3K2
Canada

www.friesenpress.com

ISBN
978-1-5255-5961-7 (Hardcover)
978-1-5255-5962-4 (Paperback)
978-1-5255-5963-1 (eBook)

1. *FICTION, HUMOROUS*
2. *FICTION, ACTION & ADVENTURE*
3. *FICTION*

Distributed to the trade by The Ingram Book Company

TABLE OF CONTENTS

CHAPTER ONE 1
A Hollywood Crucifixion

CHAPTER TWO 19
To Whom It May Concern

CHAPTER THREE 33
Sniff out the Lies

CHAPTER FOUR 65
A Whore's Panties

CHAPTER FIVE 85
A Hollow-Eyed Crack-Head

CHAPTER SIX 113
#superscasty

CHAPTER SEVEN 137
The Secret Sign

CHAPTER EIGHT 157
Deus Ex Machina

AFTERWORD 181

ABOUT THE AUTHOR 183

"In risu veritas."
— James Joyce

CHAPTER ONE

A Hollywood Crucifixion

It was going to be a hot one. Just like yesterday and the day before and the day before that. The Santa Ana winds had come early this year, carrying the bone-dry, super-heated air from the high deserts, up over the Sierras and then dumping it down onto the Los Angeles basin and the parched rock of the Hollywood Hills. Borne on the winds came the faint odour of several wildfires that raged uncontrollably across the southern half of the state, a subtle reminder that all was not well in paradise.

The two detectives stood perched on the slopes of Mount Lee, perhaps sixty feet down from the Hollywood Sign; incongruous figures in their white dress shirts, dark suit pants and city-slicker cop shoes when viewed against the backdrop of the barren terrain. The one detective, big and round and black as a bucket of Kentucky coal, resembled an ageing, overweight footballer, which was actually not too far from the truth. The other was tall and skinny, long-limbed and pale-faced, and many people had noticed his uncanny resemblance to Abraham Lincoln sans the facial hair and top hat. Despite their slightly Laurel and Hardyesque appearance, working together, they had closed more homicide cases than any other team in the history of the department. As such, Detective Sergeant William 'Beefy' Goodness (the big one) and Detective Jerome 'Leafy' Green (the skinny one) were regarded as something akin to rock stars within the ranks of the LAPD.

Both men stared up at the iconic sign, trying to make sense of the bizarre crime scene. Lodged in the nexus point of the letter Y, a young woman's naked body lay lifeless, her long, shapely legs dangling down the front of the sign. Her head and upper torso hung down at the back, obscured from the detectives' view by the sign. Chains hung from her manacled ankles, lending an air of depravity to what was already a sinister scene. Without shifting his gaze, Beefy wiped the sweat from his forehead and then wiped his hand on his trouser leg. Finally, he broke the silence.

"Man oh man. There's plain old vanilla crazy . . . ."

"And then there's California crazy."

The two had been partners for eleven and a half years, and it was not uncommon for one to finish the other's train of thought.

"Roger that," affirmed Beefy. "What are you thinking?"

"I'm thinking it's only 10:00 AM and it's already eighty-seven degrees and sure as hell the mercury will be in the triple digits by noon."

Five minutes earlier, the fire department had arrived at the top of Mount Lee. They had managed to manhandle a pair of ladders down the treacherous slope and had leaned them up against the arms of the forty-five-foot-high letter Y. As the detectives watched, the medical examiner's vehicle rolled sedately to a stop beside the fire truck.

"Looks like the ME's in no particular hurry," Beefy observed with a grimace.

"She's soaking in the last dregs of air conditioning before stepping out into this blast furnace."

"Who can blame her? Just like they say: the corpse aint gonna get any deader."

The pair trudged their way back up the slope to the epicentre of the tragedy. They had already completed an uneventful graveyard shift when this case had landed on their desk, and it was shaping up to be a long and tiring day.

The original 'Hollywoodland' sign was built as an advertisement for the real estate development of that name. Over the ensuing years, generations of Angelenos had witnessed multiple incarnations of the landmark, with the sign itself surviving numerous negative interactions with termites, arsonists, vandals and politicians, to name but a few. The modern-day sign and the surrounding area was now considered a site of important cultural heritage, with access strictly limited and the general public only able to view the sign from some distance away. The officer who had first attended the crime scene was a young LAPD patrolwoman who was stationed in nearby Griffith Park and charged with the specific task of protecting and deterring criminal behaviour on and around the sign.

"I thought you guys had this place locked up tighter than Fort Knox?" Leafy framed the statement in the tone of a rhetorical question. "What happened to all the webcams and the twenty-four-seven live monitoring and the state-of-the-art security system? Not to mention the razor-wire fence and the on-site police officer . . . ."

"Yeah," retorted the young cop, sensing the implicit criticism but unafraid despite Leafy's hallowed reputation. "Well, so has the White House, but that doesn't stop the occasional whack-job from dropping in on the President now and again. What's your point . . . Sir?"

The 'sir' was stretched out with just the merest hint of insolence, and Leafy bit back on some smartass comeback because the kid did have a good point and Leafy suddenly didn't. Instead, he pulled out his notebook and gestured for the officer to continue with her report.

"First off," the patrolwoman stated, referencing the points from her notebook. "These guys had all the required permits to be at the sign. They work for a legit company called 'The West Coast Model Agency' and they booked this photoshoot over three months ago. The deceased is a Nancy Emily Johnson, a resident of Anaheim. Apparently, she goes by — correction, went by — the stage name N. Emma Johnson."

"Enema Johnson?" interjected Beefy.

"Yeah, I know," she affirmed. "It's an unfortunate-sounding name. I think she might have been going for the J. Edgar Hoover thing. Or maybe L. Ron Hubbard."

"Elron who?"

"The Scientology guy."

"That still doesn't ring any bells," injected Beefy, scratching his head.

"How about S. Epatha Merkerson, the actor?" supplied the patrol officer, trying her best to bridge the ever-widening chasm that lay between the generations of the twenty-first century. "You know, *Law and Order*, the old-school TV show."

"Now I get you. That used to be one of my favourite shows. Still is, actually."

"O-kay." The patrolwoman stretched out the word to indicate the onset of Beefy's senility, but he either didn't notice or he ignored her derision. She continued with her report. "Even when you've got the permits and paid all the fees for a close-up event at the sign, there are pretty strict rules about what you can and can't do. Nobody's even allowed to touch the sign, never mind climb on it. One of the park staff is supposed to personally monitor all visitors for the entirety of the event."

"Supposed to?" prompted Leafy.

"This agency had booked a two-hour session, and for the first ninety minutes everything went like it normally does, with the attendant watching over things and everybody behaving themselves. Then one of the models goes up to the attendant and says she's twisted her ankle and could he help her to get back up to the car park. Him being a man and all, and her being a super-hot model in a microscopic bikini and six-inch heels . . . well, I guess he didn't need too much in the way of persuading."

"You think it was a set-up to get the watchdog off their backs for a while?" asked Beefy.

"I couldn't say for sure . . . but yeah, I think so. It was either all planned out or else the photographer just decided to go for it."

"So how did the deceased get up there?" asked Leafy.

"It's not that hard to climb up the support frame at the rear of the sign. So while the attendant was away with the supposedly injured model, Enema Johnson got naked, climbed up on the Y and somehow got shot. That's all I got. When I arrived on the scene everybody was freaking out. So apart from the park attendant, I didn't get any statements from the on-scene witnesses. When the other uniforms arrived, we herded the witnesses up to the car park and made sure nobody took off."

"All right, thanks," Leafy concluded the interview. "Stick around for a while . . . and we're going to need access to the surveillance and webcam footage."

"I've got all of the security company info on file at the park office. You can pick it up on your way out."

Leafy pulled out a quarter from his pocket, rested it on the thumb and forefinger of his right hand and smirked at his partner.

"Heads, you talk to the ME and forensics down here. Tails, I get to go interview a gaggle of gorgeous girls up there."

"Gaggle?"

"Yeah, gaggle," confirmed Leafy.

"Did you get a dictionary for your birthday or something?"

"Word of the week on my new internet browser. And lo and behold, I finally found a sentence I could use it in."

"That wild and wonderful brain of yours never stops working, does it?"

Leafy flipped the coin and won the toss, just like he always did.

"Mock all you want . . . and have fun with the ME."

* * *

Although something of a sexist cliché, it was said that beautiful women in the City of Angels were a dime a dozen and that male heterosexual construction workers — or for that matter, female homosexual construction workers — were spoiled rotten, conserving their wolf whistles and catcalls for only the most outstanding specimens. But those overindulged connoisseurs would not have held their breath with this particular group of females. Every one of them was drop-dead gorgeous, and the most beautiful of them all was undoubtedly the late N. Emma Johnson. While the others scored eights and nines on the old whistle-meter, she scored a perfect ten.

Leafy laid the glossy promotional photograph of the victim on the hood of his vehicle, lit up a cigarette and pondered his next move. He had already talked to the lovely ladies and had learned nothing of any real consequence, except that they had heard several gunshots in quick succession. None of them had seen the shooter. None of them could think of any reason why N. Emma Johnson would be killed in such a fashion. They had all really liked her and seemed genuinely shocked by her untimely demise. Additionally, none of them claimed to have foreknowledge of any plan for the deceased to climb up on the sign, including the girl with the phony sprained ankle. Leafy ground out the cigarette butt under his heel and walked across the car park to the police car where the photographer was being detained. He nodded to a uniformed officer who opened the rear door of the cruiser, allowing the witness to get out and onto his feet.

"Am I under arrest?" the young man demanded in a prissy tone Leafy really didn't much care for.

Leafy checked him out for a minute, taking in the elaborately mussed-up hairstyle, the designer jeans, the obligatory arm tattoos, the perfect suntan, the quarter-inch facial stubble and the ever-present phone clutched tightly in his right hand. He was a good-looking kid, handsome and well-built. He was also an asshole. His assholeness oozed from every pore of his body. Leafy took an instant dislike to him but he didn't let it show. After all was said and done, cops dealt with assholes on a daily basis. It was just the same old, same old. He'd seen this type a million times or more: all piss and no vinegar.

"At the moment, you are not under arrest." Leafy paused to let that news sink in. "But that could change in a heartbeat. It all depends on what you say next."

"Maybe I need a lawyer."

"Maybe you do."

"Shouldn't you or one of these other cops have read me my rights? Like, I don't have to talk to you if I don't want to, right?"

"That's right. You don't have to talk to me. Is that the way you'd like to proceed?"

"Yeah, I think so."

"Fair enough. Officer, cuff this guy and take him down to central booking."

"Wait a minute. You said I *wasn't* under arrest."

"You're not being arrested. Right now, you are a person of interest in a homicide investigation. You said you don't want to cooperate, so you'll be held for forty-eight hours in the city lockup until we decide what to do with you."

As the uniformed officer pulled out his handcuffs, the young photographer's bravado folded like a proverbial cheap suit.

"All right! Chill out a little, dude. What do you wanna know?"

Leafy decided it was time for the faux father routine.

"Listen, son . . . you seem like a good kid. I don't want to give you a hard time, but if you tell me even one little lie, I got no choice but to lock your ass up in jail. Hindering a homicide investigation is a very serious charge. A person has been murdered here . . . and you're the one who brought the deceased to her place of execution. Do you get where I'm coming from?"

"Totally. I *totally* get where you're coming from."

Leafy had been down this road before and he sensed the young man's complete and sudden desire to be compliant.

"Good. Was it your idea for Enema Johnson to climb up on the sign?"

"Yeah, it was."

"And I take it that was some kind of publicity stunt . . . like the prearranged kind of publicity stunt?"

"Yeah, I planned it out with her a couple of days ago. N. Emma Johnson was special. I took a personal interest in her career and I became her kind of unofficial manager. She was from Iowa and she had no street smarts whatsoever. If I hadn't stepped into her life she'd have been eaten alive in this town. I kept her safe."

"Yeah, you kept her safe all right," concurred Leafy, but the unsubtle irony seemed lost on the younger man. "The girl with the twisted ankle, was she in on it too?"

"No. I just asked her to do it and she went for it. She's a bit of a wingnut, if you know what I'm saying."

"And your assistant? Is he going to corroborate your story?

"Absolutely."

"So what's with the chains?"

"Plastic stage props. You know, to add a little drama to the scene. The ends of the chains have these suction cups that were supposed to stick to the sign so it looked like she was chained to it by her ankles and wrists. We were going to post the images online under the title: 'A Hollywood Crucifixion.' It would have put us on the map, no question about it. A force to be reckoned with. But I swear to God, I never thought it would turn out like this."

"I guess her being naked also added to the drama?"

"What can I tell you, bro? This is Tinseltown. You've gotta spice it up if you want to get noticed. Listen, officer, I've told you all I know. I'm sorry N. Emma Johnson's dead . . . but I *swear* I had nothing to do with her getting shot and I have no idea who would've wanted to hurt her. The whole thing just doesn't make sense. I mean, she was just a sweet little country girl trying to make it in the city. Can I go now?"

"Yeah, you and the girls can take off. We've got your contact info and we may have some more questions for you. Make sure you're available if I call."

As the photographer turned towards his vehicle another question occurred to the detective.

"There's one more thing I gotta ask you. Was it you that came up with the name Enema Johnson?"

"Yeah, I did."

"Now for *that* you should be arrested."

* * *

Over the years, psychological studies had been conducted on the effects of the Santa Ana winds on the minds of people. It had been statistically proven that an increase in the rates of suicides and homicides was directly linked to those periods when the winds were active and that the amount of that increase was directly proportional to the winds' duration and strength. But for the average Californian, those less prone to extreme acts of violence, the effects of the Santa Ana winds were somewhat more subtle. Irritability, anxiety and depression were generally recognised as the chief symptoms associated with this meteorological aberration.

Leafy sat behind the wheel of their unmarked Crown Victoria, air conditioner cranked and blasting full in his face. For whatever reason, he was feeling irritable, anxious and slightly depressed, and he put it down to a lack of sleep and an empty belly. The car sat stationary beside the park office and he watched through the windshield as Beefy finally concluded a series of phone calls and headed back towards the vehicle. The large detective eased his weight onto the passenger seat and slammed the door shut.

"Damn! That's crazy hot out there."

"There's nothing like stating the obvious," Leafy quipped, sounding irritable, anxious and slightly depressed.

"I know, I know. But damn! That's crazy hot out there."

Leafy placed his hand on the gearshift and his foot on the brake.

"Are we done here?"

"Yeah, I think we've ticked off all the boxes," affirmed Beefy as he studied his notes.

Leafy shifted into drive and headed back down the mountain, listening carefully as his partner began to rhyme off what he had gleaned thus far in the case.

"Okay, let's see now . . . the Iowa State Troopers are notifying the next of kin. They'll check things out at their end and see if there's a hometown connection to the case. Could be there's some farm boy back in Iowa pissed off that his beauty-queen girlfriend dumped him and then took off to Hollywood to find fame and fortune. If anything comes up, they'll let us know. The Digital Forensics Unit is on its way over to pick up the webcam and surveillance video hard-drive data from the security company. Hopefully they should have something to show us by mid-afternoon. Now, you know how much Angelina hates to go out on a limb . . . ."

"*You two boys will just have to learn to be patient and wait for the autopsy,*" Leafy mimicked in a creditable imitation of the formidable Latino medical examiner.

"Yeah, well, in this particular case, you don't need a degree in pathology to figure out the cause of death: a single gunshot wound fired from a medium-calibre long gun. The round entered from the front through her left lower ribcage and exited from her right shoulder blade. Angelina said the victim would have bled out in a matter of seconds."

"Any chance the bullet's still in the body?"

"She said she'll fast track the autopsy, but judging from the size of the exit wound, it would be best not to hold our breaths on that one. She also said it reminded her of a battlefield wound: straight in and straight out, no matter what's in the way. And you know what that probably means . . . ."

"Steel-jacketed military round, possibly NATO but not US. Probably Warsaw Pact."

The United States military had long since adopted the relatively small .223 calibre as the standard infantry rifle round. Most European NATO forces had similarly changed over from the 7.62mm to the 5.56mm round, which was effectively the metric equivalent of the two-twenty-three. These decisions had been made during the Cold War, when the military planners had felt that the infantry would either be fighting at close quarters with the communists in the densely packed cities of Europe or in the confined jungles of Vietnam. The slightly less powerful round was much lighter than its predecessors and enabled the average infantryman to carry a lot more ammunition onto the field of battle. Armies of the former Soviet Empire, however, had stuck steadfastly to the tried and tested 7.62mm ammo, which had a longer range, was less susceptible to deflection and imparted more kinetic energy onto the target than its western counterpart. Mandated by the Geneva Convention, most armies of the world now use steel-jacketed ammunition because of its tendency to pass straight through the human body and thus reduce the medical complications associated with bullet fragmentation and infection. Both ex-military men, this was all second nature to the two detectives.

Leafy continued his train of thought. "Then unless it's a hunting rifle or an obsolete NATO gun — which we don't really see that much of on the streets of LA — it has to be that good old weapon of choice for both terrorists and gangbangers alike: an AK-47."

"You betcha! And as we don't really get too much in the way of terrorism around here, that might mean we've got some kind of gang connection. How does that fit in with the victim's lifestyle?"

"From what I've been told, it doesn't fit in at all. If you believe what the other girls say, Enema Johnson was just a sweet, innocent young girl. No drugs, no alcohol, no bad habits . . . just lots of fun and easy to get along with. A veritable saint."

"It's still early days in the case," offered Beefy, "and we're just bouncing around a few ideas. We'll stick the gang thing on the back burner for now, subject to future confirmation."

"Is there any good news? Anything solid that we can get our teeth into right now?"

Beefy consulted his notes.

"CSI found a total of five bullet holes in the sign. Four of them show signs of weathering and had been fired from completely different angles. What is it about signs that people love to shoot at them? Anyway, they've got nothing to do with Enema Johnson's murder. The fifth hole is brand-spanking new, maybe five feet lower than the killing round and penetrating the first L of 'Hollywood.' Actually, it's two holes — an entry and an exit from the same projectile at the front and back of the sign — and forensics have got an approximate fix on the position of the shooter by laser-sighting back along the trajectory of the holes. Uniforms are already searching with metal detectors above and below the sign for casings or projectiles. The K9 unit is on the way with propellant-sniffing dogs. If there's anything out there, we should be able to find it. That's all I got so far. What's the story on the witnesses?"

"They didn't tell me much I didn't already know," explained Leafy, with little in the way of enthusiasm. "Enema Johnson moved to the LA area about six months ago. She shares a small apartment with two other girls in Anaheim. She worked part-time as a waitress at a sushi restaurant near Angel Stadium. She's dated a few guys but has no regular boyfriend. She wanted to be a successful model. All pretty standard stuff, nothing too exciting. The photographer's just another LA schmuck trying to take advantage of the young hopefuls. He admitted to planning out the sign-climbing thing as a publicity stunt — apparently the city is gonna be laying charges for that at a later date — but he definitely aint no killer. Besides, who in their right mind would set up a hit in such a public place in front of so many witnesses? The problem I got with this whole case right now, Beefy, is that I'm just not getting the *motive*. I feel like we're flogging a dead horse."

"Isn't it feeding a dead horse?" offered Beefy. "Or maybe it's fooling?" "I thought it was flogging, but now that I think about it, it could be fondling."

"I know this much: you can lead a dead horse to water, but you can't make it sink."

"Really? I thought it was: You can fondle a dead horse in the water, but you can't make it think."

"No way, José. I'm pretty darned sure it's: You can feed a dead horse in the water, but you can't make it shrink."

"You know what, Beefy? They're all donaldishly effective in their own special way."

"Very, very true."

While it was not necessary to prove a motive for murder to attain a successful prosecution in a court of law, a successful conclusion to a murder investigation could be very difficult to achieve without knowing the reason behind the crime. The motive defined the direction of the case and served to narrow down the list of suspects. In Leafy and Beefy's world, motivation for murder fell into four general categories: Love, Money, Grudge or Crazy, in descending order of likelihood and solvability. There was also another somewhat esoteric category that they had labelled Political, but that had never come up on their watch. Due to their random and sometimes incomprehensible nature, cases in the Crazy category were always the hardest to close.

"There's no reason in the world why this girl should be dead," continued Leafy. "If she fell off the sign and broke her neck, I'd get that. If she was stabbed during a mugging, I'd get that. If she was shot during a robbery at the sushi restaurant, I'd get that. If she was kidnapped and murdered by a sexual predator, I'd even get that. Something aint right here, and I'm already starting to get a bad feeling about this case."

"Don't say that, man! You're gonna jinx the case right from the start. Let's just concentrate on the 'who, what, where and when.' We'll worry about the 'why' later."

"Yeah, you're right. Sorry about that. I retract my previous statement. We're good to go and there is no jinx. Everything's totally cool and the case is still fresh as a daisy and completely un-jinxed. Is that good enough for you?"

"You know the rules, Leafy," chided Beefy. "Once something's been jinxed you can't just un-jinx the jinx at the drop of a hat. You gotta run with the jinx. Chill with the jinx. Maybe have a few beers with the jinx, get to know the jinx's family. And then, when you've gained the jinx's confidence and you're up close and personal and the jinx is sleepy and off guard . . . *that's* when you un-jinx the jinx."

"Let's go get something to eat."

Of the two detectives, Beefy, at the age of forty-nine, was the senior man. He had the sergeant's stripes, with almost twenty years of service with the department and experience in specialized police units other than homicide. Leafy, on the other hand, was forty-two years old, had never bothered to apply for promotion, had a thirteen-year service record and had transitioned directly from being a humble patrol officer to the homicide bureau.

Leafy had been a first-year rookie detective when the powers-that-be had decided, in their infinite wisdom, to join him and Beefy at the hip. Leafy's first impressions of Beefy had been that his new partner was an arrogant and humourless know-it-all. Beefy, for his part, had protested long and hard to his superiors, citing Leafy's overall disre-spect for authority and generally frivolous nature as the main areas of incompatibility; but it was all to no avail. There was no appeals process when it came to the assignment of employees within the department, and unless Leafy stepped over the line through either incompetence or misconduct, Beefy would have to suck it up and somehow make the partnership work.

Eleven and a half years later, Leafy had never stepped over that line, although he had come close a few times. He was too smart for that. Beefy now realized that under his partner's oftentimes impermeable layer of superficiality there lay hidden a highly disciplined individual dedicated to the apprehension of violent criminals. So, over the years an initial dislike of each other had slowly metamorphosed through several stages of pupation, from grim acceptance to grudging respect to professional tolerance to tacit admiration to genuine friendship and then on to the ultimate goal of any positive relationship: unwavering trust.

Even though they sometimes disagreed, even about agreeing to disagree, both detectives wholeheartedly agreed that they weren't always disagreeable. And on very rare occasions, they agreed to be as agreeable as possible without appearing to be disagreeable on matters that they had previously agreed to disagree upon, unless that matter was so utterly disagreeable that they had no choice but to agree.

Both men acknowledged privately and to each other that their unlikely partnership was the real key to their success as investigators and that their oftentimes polarized viewpoints, when combined, allowed for a much wider and deeper field of vision. The differences in their personalities remained to this day. But the overlapping area that had become their common ground might best be summed up with the introduction of an imaginary, melded persona of the two, which for descriptive purposes could be called Bleefy.

While Leafy was a slightly left of centre democrat; a navy veteran; a confirmed smoker; a consumer of unhealthy foods who never gained weight; a twice-divorced man who expressed disbelief in the American dream; a lover of rock and roll music and also a jovial pessimist. Beefy, on the other hand, was a slightly right of centre republican; an army veteran; a rabid anti-smoker; a consumer of healthy foods who never seemed to lose weight; a happily married family man who believed in the American dream; a lover of country and western music and also a serious optimist. The blended Bleefy character, however, was wary of politicians of all stripes; pro-military; had flexible rules about second-hand smoke; couldn't care less what people ate or their body mass index; did not delve too deeply into other people's private lives; was fiercely patriotic and was an enlightened sceptic. Additionally, Bleefy had sympathy for the underdog, tolerance for minorities and a degree of empathy for just about everybody on the planet except for cold-blooded murderers.

Additionally, Bleefy no longer believed in God anymore, at least not in the image portrayed by the major religions. The idea of a just and compassionate deity solely dedicated to the welfare of mankind was an absurd concept, given the number of violent atrocities that both men had witnessed over the course of their military and police careers. Putting freedom of speech and twenty-first century 'enlightenment' aside, Leafy and Beefy were well aware that such a profession of disbelief would not be well received by those around them and both men kept their iconoclastic views a closely guarded secret. Even their families had no idea about their atheism, and whenever he could, Beefy still dutifully attended church services with his wife and kids, quietly resolved that he would not be the one responsible for bursting his family's religious bubble. To Beefy, the myth of God was something akin to Santa Claus or the Tooth Fairy, and his family would either grow out of it or they would not. On the flip side of the equation, both men understood mankind's age-old desire to find meaning in its existence with the creation of a Creator and the comforting promise of an afterlife when faced with the awful finality of death.

Furthermore, the melded persona Bleefy did not believe in the concept of luck and the implicit suggestion that certain individuals possessed some intangible reservoir of good or bad fortune that the rest of humanity did not. Again, Bleefy empathised with the temptation to attribute the successes and failures of human existence to some underlying supernatural force. Why is that guy richer than me? Why did she get the promotion and I got left behind? Why am I such a thing of beauty when she looks like the back end of a Greyhound bus? Why did kind and gentle Uncle Bob have to die in a multi-vehicle freeway pile-up when infamous serial-killers live on in prison to taunt us with their twisted views of life? As far as Bleefy was concerned, the events of life — both good and bad — occurred in an entirely random fashion, and confirmation of this viewpoint was never better illustrated than on the field of battle.

In his first tour in Afghanistan, Leafy had been riding shotgun in a Humvee as part of a convoy of vehicles resupplying an outlying firebase. The army EOD guys had declared that stretch of the highway to be clear of Taliban explosives, and a total of eleven military vehicles had already passed with impunity over the exact same spot where Leafy's Humvee was blown apart. Although Leafy could not remember the actual explosion, he did recall regaining consciousness on the floor of the medi-vac helicopter with a splitting concussion headache and a badly bitten tongue. Along with some scratches on his face and hands, that was the full extent of his injuries. The Marine driver and the two army guys hitching a ride in the back of the Humvee, however, had not fared so well. All three had died instantly, their bodies torn asunder into a multitude of barely recognizable chunks of flesh and bone. It was on that short chopper ride that Leafy had ceased to believe in both God and luck. His reasoning was simple and, as far as he was concerned, unassailable. In his heart, Leafy knew that he himself was nothing special, that he was just like the Joe Walsh song: an ordinary, average guy. He was also fairly certain that his three fallen comrades would probably have characterised themselves in much the same way. Therefore, there was no reason to believe that he possessed some well of good fortune that had somehow kept him alive just as there was no reason to believe that his fallen comrades had some well of misfortune that had made them dead. It had been a completely random event with no underlying rhyme or reason. So, if God and luck did not exist during the harsh conditions of combat — when it could be argued that a person might need them the most — then it seemed only natural to both Leafy and Beefy that neither God nor luck exerted any influence over the events of everyday life.

But quite perversely, the two detectives believed very strongly in the power of the jinx, which, by the mere utterance of certain sentiments — overly pessimistic or overly optimistic — the outcome of any situation could be influenced in a negative way. To reconcile this deviation from their avowed creed of randomness, they viewed the jinx as more of a self-fulfilling prophecy that in turn leant more towards the psychological than the mystical.

These latter philosophical ruminations had occurred several years ago when they were just getting to know each other, in a seedy watering hole near the Port of LA after a few liberal shots of tequila had loosened the detectives' tongues. The subject had never been brought up again, as they felt that their conclusions spoke for themselves. And unless something came up that might change their minds, there was nothing to be gained by restating the case. In general, Leafy and Beefy preferred to keep their conversations on a lighter level, reserving the serious talk for the job in hand. One of their unspoken, but clearly understood, rules of behaviour was that there would be no talking shop at meal times.

CHAPTER TWO

To Whom It May Concern

In a small eatery in the Arts District, the two detectives sat across the table from each other, digesting their lunches and sipping on what remained of their beverages. The waitress arrived with their separate checks. Beefy's showed a chicken salad with low-fat dressing, a glass of OJ and a black coffee; Leafy's a double quarter-pounder with extra cheese, large fries and three sodas. Leafy reached for a pick and proceeded to remove the remaining morsels of junk-food debris from between his teeth. Finally, he broke their ruminative silence.

"You'll never guess who I met up with the other day."

Beefy had heard the same opening line a thousand times before and knew it was the prelude to one of Leafy's outlandish celebrity stories. He also knew that once his partner had uttered the opening line, nothing short of an extreme geological event could deter him from finishing his story. So as usual, with little option to do otherwise, Beefy played along.

"Let's see now . . . what was that guy's name who starred in *Stop Gun?* You know, that short SOB with the aviator glasses and the heroic schnozzle . . . ."

"Nope, it wasn't Tom. I'm pretty sure he quit acting and has since moved on to bigger and better things as second-in-command of that brainwashing, pseudo-scientific, anti-psychiatry, holy-roller cult over on Sunset Boulevard."

"Is that a fact? Then who's that other knucklehead? The one with all the muscles . . . got himself into politics, for God's sake."

"Arnold? He's been in rehab for the last eighteen months, but apparently there's really no hope for him. He'll never lose the accent. Right now there's a Hollywood look-alike doing all his public engagements, and the funny thing is nobody can tell the difference. Not even his wife."

"That's too bad. Apart from the wiener-schnitzel voice, he seems like such a stand-up kinda guy."

"That's very true. Isn't it weird how bad things always seem to happen to good people? My grandma always used to say: 'It's always *nice* when something *nice* happens to *nice* people.'"

"Your grandma sounds like a really *nice* person," commented Beefy. "So who did you see?"

"Keef-freaking-Richass!"

"Get outta here!"

"Seriously, man, it's true. He was thumbing a ride down on the Strip, guitar case in hand. He's getting on a bit now. Not exactly the spring chicken he used to be. So I pulled over and picked him up and he asks me if I know where Tom Revolta's house is at, for pity's sakes. So I says, 'Keefie baby, you don't wanna be hanging round with the likes of old Tommy Revolta. He'll just get a sweet little English dude like you into a whole mess of trouble. Besides, I'm pretty sure TR took off in his jumbo jet to Florida to start up a python-farm franchise in the everglades.'"

"Okay, I'll bite," said Beefy, polishing off the last swig of his orange juice. "Python-farm franchise?"

"I don't know too much about them . . . but apparently, they manage to capture the pythons initially as an invasive species at a very low overhead and then sell them back to their country of origin at over a thousand per cent mark-up. After a while, the country of origin reclassifies the invasive species as an endangered species by virtue of their deforestation programs and consequent animal habitat loss and they then sell them back to the American zoos at an even higher profit margin. With each transaction, thousands of carbon credits are accrued and subsequently cashed in for digital currency which are in turn converted into diamonds, gold and good, old US dollars. The cycle is continued over and over again until you really don't know what to do with all your money. And any spare pythons left over are distributed to various discreet slaughterhouses, which then redistribute the meat to fast-fry chicken outlets across the country. I'm told that the pythons taste more like chicken than chickens do. It's a classic win-win situation."

"It's the *American Way*," Beefy affirmed, with italicised patriotic pride. "That kinda reminds me of that innovative company importing glow-in-the-dark seafood — the kind that shouldn't normally glow in the dark — from the Marshall Islands. I think they're called the Irradiated Marshall Island Seafood Company, but don't quote me on that. The reddest red snappers you've ever seen on your plate. To die for! And apparently, just one sea-cucumber caught within a hundred mile radius of the Runit Dome will light up an average-sized American household for a couple of weeks."

"What a brilliant idea! I bet those Marshall Islanders are just brimming with gratitude for all of the environmental assistance the US has given them since the end of World War Two. Anyhow . . . I says to Keef: 'Listen, Keef, I know you're new in town and LA can be a pretty lonely place, but I gotta talk to you about that cameo role you played in that pirate movie. I mean, come on, man, it wasn't good. It so wasn't good that I cringed in embarrassment for you. My wife cringed, my kids cringed, my pet hamster cringed. I bet even the rest of the band-members must have taken a ride into Cringeville too.' Now, I was just trying to help the guy out, Beefy. A little reality check, a nudge in the right direction. You know what I'm saying?"

"If more people were as caring as you, this world would be a much better place. So what did he say to all that?"

"Absolutely nothing. It turns out he was packing heat. So he jams this three-fifty-seven snub-nose in my ribs and tells me to take him to La Guardia. So I says, 'Keef, don't you mean LAX?' He looks at me with this kind of befuddled look . . . ."

"Befuddled?"

"Yeah, befuddled. So he reaches into his fanny pack to check out what's written on his plane tickets. That's when I used this old trick I learnt when I was one of Uncle Sam's Misguided Children. The first part of the trick is called: distract the enemy and grab his weapon."

"That's a neat trick. So what happened then?"

"I put all six rounds into the upper part of his body. That's the *second* part of the trick. You gotta understand, after all those years of training it was a purely reflexive reaction. And besides, Beefy, it wasn't just the cameo thing that was pissing me off. I still remember his first solo album."

"Really? I'm not a rock and roll guy, but I thought it was pretty damned good. It showed off both his considerable musical talent and well-seasoned multi-styled versatility without making too much of a giant fuss about it all. Anyway, it looks like you did the world a very small favour and saved old Keef from any future embarrassment. What did you do with his body?"

"For sanitary reasons, I dropped it off at the morgue. It turned out to be quite a party that night. In fact, I've never seen the mortuary staff in such high spirits. We all cut off a lock of Keef's hair to keep as a souvenir — I tell you, man, it was quite a touching moment — and then we downloaded a bunch of old rock and roll tunes, broke out the secret booze stash and boogied the night away. The last I saw of Keef, he was being spun around on a gurney to the opening riff of 'Slime is on My Side' . . . or was it 'Stumbling Mice'? I don't know, I was pretty ripped by then. I heard through the grapevine that the other band members are all pitching in for a decent burial at sea."

"Don't tell me. The 'Davy Jones' Locker' thing, right?"

"You got it. It's only fitting, Beefy. Let the punishment fit the crime."

"Leafy, did I ever mention that there's a fair to strong possibility that you might have been dropped on the head as an infant? And now, you're what we normal people refer to as: damaged in transit."

"Yeah, I'm pretty sure you have mentioned that particular possibility when I come to think about it. But you gotta understand, that as a general rule, I don't like to burden my brain with too many thoughts 'cause I read somewhere that that can be really harmful to the neurons."

"What do you reckon?" asked Beefy, as he rose to his feet. "Shall we put the old nose to the grindstone again?"

"Let's do it."

The two left a collective tip, paid individually for their lunches and headed back out onto the scorched, desert-dry streets of LA.

* * *

DNA evidence was often touted as the latest and greatest weapon in the forensic investigator's arsenal. Endorsed by the scientific community and now universally accepted by the courts, the police, the general public and even the criminals themselves as irrefutable proof of any given individual's close contact with an object, person or location. Even in its early days, DNA had proven a most useful prosecutorial tool; and now, with the huge advances in technology, tests could be conducted on the minutest of biological samples, and the tests themselves were cheaper, faster and more accurate.

But like everything else in this world, DNA evidence was not perfect. Some of the problems lay in the DNA itself. It was fragile and easily destroyed or degraded by such factors as weather, water immersion, excessive heat, cross contamination and general mishandling of the evidentiary samples. And despite a plethora of TV shows portraying the contrary, DNA was not really applicable to the majority of criminal cases. Additionally, the police could have in their possession the most pristine sample of DNA, but just like a fingerprint, still have no viable suspect for comparison. Both Leafy and Beefy found DNA to be wonderful stuff, yet somewhat limited in its scope. But for the biggest bang for your buck, the real breakthrough in criminology, and the one that could be applied to the widest variety of cases, had to be the arrival of the digital revolution.

In one form or another, just about everybody on the planet — from goatherds in Mongolia to bag ladies in Peru to the masters of the universe on Wall Street — had signed on to the brave, new digital world. In fact, even the most fanatical of Luddites had to go to extraordinary lengths to escape the technological world's tenacious grip. Computers, the internet, social media, GPS, surveillance cameras, data banks and especially cell phones were just some of the delicious morsels available to law-enforcement agencies in the veritable smörgasbord of digitization. Beefy had best summed up his thoughts on the subject of cell phones in the conclusion of a seminar that he had given to the latest batch of graduates at the police academy last year entitled: *Do you have access to the internet? Or does the internet have access to you?*

"Picture this, ladies and gentlemen: the federal government — with the full backing of both houses of congress — enacts a law mandating that every man, woman and child in the country has to carry a personal electronic tracking device so that the government can know where each and every citizen is at any given moment. Personal information relating to identity, banking data, names and addresses of family and friends and several other parameters must be stored within this tracking device. Furthermore, all communications and captured visual images must be carried out with this device so that this information can be harvested and stored in meta-data banks for future governmental scrutiny. Sounds like something George Orwell might come up with, right? What do you think would happen if the government really tried to pass such a law? I'll *tell* you what would happen. Everybody, from the ACLU to the NRA to the NAACP, would flip out about the erosion of civil liberties and the destruction of our constitutional rights, and the country would be faced with something close to insurrection. But of course the powers-that-be are way too smart to try to pass a crazy law like that. If nothing else, just imagine how expensive it would be to equip everybody in America with a tracking device. Far better to outsource the project, allowing private corporations to sell the wonders of digitization to the general public by emphasising the numerous side-line benefits, while at the same time playing down the aspect of Big Brother knowing their every move. Now despite Edward Snowden's and WikiLeaks' revelations and the fact that millions of US citizens have had their personal information compromised through corporate hacking attacks to the tune of many billions of dollars, the general public continues to view cell phones as an essential staple of life in the twenty-first century. Let's face it: cell phones are just too useful and convenient to resist. Emphasis on the word *convenient*. I myself am a cell phone addict. But then again, I do not store unnecessary personal information on my device and neither do I carry out sensitive transactions over the internet. In fact, my digital profile would make for very tedious reading, both for the NSA analysts and the hackers alike. Which brings me to my main point: not everybody is as cautious as I am when it comes to cell phone communication. Because of this inability to perceive the immense vulnerability of cell phones and other electronic devices — which I have come to call 'digital blindness' — most people under the age of forty-five unwittingly carry around in their back pockets a virtual treasure trove of useful information for law-enforcement officers across the country. Sometimes their phones actually contain a record of their whole life. Of course, the rules of evidence still apply and warrants are required to obtain digital information . . . but if a subject waives his or her rights and consents to a phone check, or if a device appears to have been lost or discarded, then that's a completely different matter. You would be amazed how much information, incriminating and otherwise, people forget is even on their phones. Anyhow, that about wraps this up. Thank you for your time. Now get out there and catch some bad guys!"

The Digital Forensics Unit was located some thirty feet below ground level in the sub-basement of a city-owned archival warehouse just a few blocks south of the downtown area. Due to the ever-rising demand for its services, the unit was undergoing a complete refit of its equipment and infrastructure and the place was presently a scene of highly organized chaos. Tradesmen and technicians of every variety stomped their way through the narrow corridors as Leafy and Beefy picked their way through the obstacle course to room 101. Beefy pressed a button on the numeric keypad on the wall beside the door and offered a cheesy smile to the enigmatic dome of the surveillance camera. The electronic lock clicked open and the two entered the room.

"Bill! Jerry! What's going on in the land of the surface dwellers?"

Detective Armand Hammer was at the forefront of a new breed of super-nerd, tech-head cops whose job it was to patrol the dark highways and byways of the electronic world in search of digital evidence and cyber criminals. Although he had been acquainted with Leafy and Beefy for less than six months, he always greeted them like they were long-lost friends. With his baby face and omnipresent smile, Leafy and Beefy had privately characterised the twenty-six-year-old Armand Hammer as being an incurably and insanely happy policeman. But the most important thing to the two detectives was that he was also extremely good at his job.

"You know how it is with us surface dwellers, Armand," replied Leafy, engaging in Hammer's conversational theme. "Never a dull moment. How's life in the Bat Cave treating you?"

"Absolutely wonderful! In another two weeks I get to play with a whole bunch of new toys courtesy of the department, and the Bat Cave will return to its normal peace and quiet. I also heard through the grapevine that the Cyber Crimes Division is going to be merging with the Digital Forensic Unit. And *guess* who's going to be in charge."

"Way to go, Armand. You deserve a promotion," Beefy responded, courteous, but determined to stay on point. "So . . . what have you got for us?"

In most cases that involved video evidence it was rare to have more than one camera covering the actual crime itself, and both Leafy and Beefy were quite capable of setting up a viewing on their own computers in the Homicide Division offices. In the case of N. Emma Johnson, however, there happened to be an abundance of cameras covering the scene from a multitude of angles, and several synchronized video monitors would be required in order to gain a real-time perspective of the situation as a whole.

Armand Hammer glanced down at his notes and got down to the business at hand.

"There's a lot of footage, I can tell you guys that much. Out of a total of seventeen cameras, three were malfunctioning. The data from the remaining fourteen varies from high-definition to ultra-grainy. There are five different views of the victim's final moments. The other nine cameras offer pan and wide-angle shots of the scene or are targeted at specific locations such as the car parks and security gates. I already went through the photographer's still shots, but they're mostly close-ups of the models. Easy on the eye, but I doubt they'll be much use to you in the investigation. Two of the webcams were equipped with microphones, but they are mounted some distance from the scene and the quality of the audio is compromised by wind and ambient city noise. As always, the Donald is in the details."

"Okay," said Beefy. "Let's start with those five views of the victim . . . let's say, ten minutes before she got shot. Crank up the audio and get ready to hit the freeze button, Armand."

Armand sat down at his workstation, well-practised fingers flying across the keyboard at warp speed. A huge bank of monitors lined the wall behind the workstation and, with a final tap on the Enter key, the first five came to life offering frontal, rear and elevated views of the Hollywood Sign. An air of tension descended upon the room as the three police officers locked their collective attention on the events unfolding on the screens. They had watched videos like this before and they knew how profoundly disturbing it was to actually witness a victim's speedy and oftentimes brutal transition from the land of the living to the absolute nothingness of death.

Leafy took up the commentary.

"There's our victim. There's photographer-boy and that's his assistant standing next to him with the lighting rig."

The photo session appeared to be taking a break and the bikini-clad girls stood around, taking sips from their water bottles, checking their phones and generally goofing off.

"Oh yeah, here we go! Photographer-boy is taking sprained-ankle-girl aside for a private moment. Now she's headed for the park attendant . . . and *down* she goes. Park attendant is running over and helping her to her feet. And sure enough, off they go up the hill together just like photographer-boy said."

At that moment, the scene changed from one of relaxation to one of furious activity. N. Emma Johnson deftly slipped off her bathing suit and shed her high heels. She donned a pair of flip-flops and ran naked to the base of the letter Y. The photographer's assistant removed the plastic chains from a bag and attached them to her ankles and wrists.

One thing was transparently clear from the videos: N. Emma Johnson was a willing participant in this crazy stunt and appeared to be having the time of her life. With athletic ease and not a hint of self-consciousness, she mounted the support frame and began to climb. She said something to the photographer's assistant but the microphones were too far away to pick up the words. The sound of the audio track was an irritating cacophony of deep rumbles, distant traffic noise and emergency vehicle sirens in the city. When the victim was about halfway between the ground and the nexus point of the Y, Beefy yelled to Armand to freeze the action.

"Did you guys hear that?" queried Beefy. "Roll it back, Armand. And can you filter out some of that low-end noise?"

Armand Hammer made the necessary adjustments and brought up the sound-analyser screen on his personal monitor. He hit the play button and once again N. Emma Johnson donned her chains and began her fateful ascent of the support frame. This time there was no mistaking the sound of an automatic weapon being fired, albeit some distance from the sign.

"Look at their faces," Beefy observed. "No reaction to the gunshots. Nobody even batted an eyelid."

"The acoustic signature is consistent with a high-velocity firearm," Armand confirmed. "I got eight peaks on the graph. Consequently, it was an eight-round burst."

The tension in the room ratcheted up a couple of notches as N. Emma Johnson stepped from the support frame onto the sign and sat down between the arms of the Y. With a triumphant smile, the raven-haired beauty waved to her admiring audience below. At that moment, another volley of shots — louder and longer than the first — sounded from the audio speakers.

"Thirteen-round burst," supplied Armand.

This time, several of the witnesses turned their heads to look down the mountain, including N. Emma Johnson, whose high-spirited smile had transformed into an expression of mild concern. Another single shot rang out followed by two more in quick succession and N. Emma Johnson was knocked flat on her back into precisely the same position the two detectives had found her only hours before. In a matter of seconds, a dark spreading stain appeared on the sign below the victim as the lifeblood drained from her body. Several screams sounded from the crowd below when they finally grasped the shocking brutality of what had just occurred.

"Shut it down, Armand," said Beefy, shaking his head. "Man oh man. We don't get paid enough to watch this sort of stuff."

"That's a big ten-four," Leafy agreed. "Just imagine how the President feels having to watch those Situation-Room snuff movies as the special-ops teams execute the terrorist head-honchos in real time while he's munching down on an extra-large portion of extra-cheesy popcorn and tweeting out the spoiler-highlights of the state-sanctioned assassination to all and sundry."

"Yeah, it must be tough," put in Armand Hammer. "And it's no wonder he has a cholesterol-slash-calcium problem. But by not trying them in a court of law, Jerry, it saves the Justice Department a bunch of aggravation and the American taxpayer a whole heck of a lot of money. Not to mention that there are far less repercussions if we forgo all that pesky right-to-a-fair-trial legal stuff and just dump their bodies in the ocean."

Beefy had a daughter just a couple of years younger than the victim, and for a few short moments, he contemplated how it would feel to lose her in such a terrible fashion. He knew from experience, however, that it was huge mistake for an investigator to become emotionally involved in a case and he shoved those thoughts to the back of his mind.

"So what have we got?" he asked, semi-rhetorically. "Two bursts of automatic fire and three single shots on semi-auto for a total of . . . ."

"Twenty-four," Armand interjected.

"Twenty-four rounds expended and one hit. Not exactly the best shooting score in the world."

"I don't know," commented Leafy. "I'd say that's about par for the course. Most of the trigger-happy idiots we arrest are not exactly sniper material."

"That's very true. I guess there's only one way to get an ID on the shooter. Intermission is over, Armand. Let's roll the second half of today's featured matinee."

"Already cued and ready to go, Bill," said Armand, efficient as ever. "Do you want the audio track at the same volume level?"

"Most definitely. Okay, we've got nine cameras left, so let's split up the workload and watch three monitors apiece. Otherwise, we're going to be here for the rest of the day."

With a final keystroke from Armand, monitors six through fourteen came to life, revealing the crime scene from entirely different perspectives to the previous viewing.

"Shut down number twelve. It's just the upper car park," Leafy commanded.

"Ditto on nine and eleven," Beefy chimed in, whittling the task down to six monitors. "We don't need the main gates and access road."

The detectives were now quite certain that the shooter had been located some distance below and to the east of the Hollywood Sign; and those were the money-shots that interested them the most. The first burst of gunfire crackled from the speakers, but nothing untoward appeared on the screens. As the second round of shots began, Armand froze the screens.

"I've got movement on number seven," he reported, while simultaneously rewinding the video a few frames.

The three gathered around monitor seven and Armand resumed the play function. This particular camera was mounted somewhere beside the D in 'Hollywood' and offered a panoramic view down across the slopes of Mount Lee with the city as a backdrop. Once again, the second burst of gunfire sounded and the figure of a man appeared at the bottom left-hand side of the screen running full tilt across the side of the mountain. Small fountains of rock and dirt erupted all around him, each eruption closely synchronized with the sounds of the gunshots. After all twenty-four shots had been expended, the figure appeared to be miraculously unharmed and eventually disappeared from view at the bottom right-hand side of the screen. Leafy got Armand to replay the remaining five videos to be absolutely sure they had not missed anything, but only monitor seven captured the runner's wild dash across the mountain. Unfortunately, there was no sign of the shooter.

Without prompting, Armand had already located a single frame of the running-man that showed the man's face turned up towards the camera and he zoomed in for a more detailed close-up shot. The resulting image was surprisingly good, and it revealed a short, stocky man in his mid-to-late fifties with an unkempt beard and a thick mop of long, white hair that was faintly reminiscent of Albert Einstein. He was wearing a dirty yellow T-shirt two sizes too big for him and a pair of ragged jeans. A small, blue knapsack hung from his shoulders and his heavily lined features fully reflected the terrifying situation that he was experiencing at that particular moment. It seemed fairly obvious that this was one of the many thousands of homeless people that roamed the streets of LA.

Before anybody could comment, the Dragnet-theme ringtone of Leafy's phone cut through the silence and a brief conversation ensued.

"That was forensics. They recovered shell casings and bullet fragments from the scene. The ejector marks on the casings almost certainly came from an AK-47 and the rounds used were steel-jacketed, military specification. They're running comparisons on the casings through the database to see if the gun's been used in other local crimes. They should have some preliminary results within the hour. A wider national search might take a few days."

"Well, I guess that about wraps things up in the Bat Cave, Armand," said Beefy, moving towards the door. "If you could enhance that picture of the running-man and send a copy over to the office, we surface dwellers would be eternally grateful."

"You got it, Bill. I hope you guys aren't too disappointed that we didn't get a visual on the killer."

"We're leaving with more than when we arrived," Leafy replied. "The witnesses' stories check out okay. We have a pretty good picture of the intended victim. And last, but by no means least, we now know that Enema Johnson died for no reason at all. She was just collateral damage."

"It's like we always said in the infantry," intoned Beefy. "It's not the bullet with your name on it you should worry about. It's the ones that are addressed: *To Whom It May Concern*."

CHAPTER THREE

Sniff out the Lies

After a gruelling twenty-hour shift the previous day, Leafy and Beefy had finally called it quits and gone home to their beds to rest their bodies and recalibrate their brains.

It was now 7:00 AM and the two stood in a corner of the homicide division office watching the new coffeemaker hiss and spit through its final stages of percolation. The office was well equipped when it came to caffeine-laced beverage dispensers, and the new machine stood at the end of a long line of similar machines that could make anything from authentic Italian espresso to the most exotic of international flavours. This new one, however, was a commercial machine of the sort that might be found in a restaurant and it was as ruggedly built as an Abrams tank. Connected through a filter directly to the building's water supply, it had cost a small fortune to purchase and have installed — paid for out of Leafy and Beefy's own pockets — and it produced the quickest, hottest and most satisfying pot of medium-roast java that had ever been consumed within the homicide office. The new coffeemaker was a big hit with the other detectives, and Leafy and Beefy basked in their colleagues' praise at the wisdom of their new investment. The other detectives were welcome to use it, but it was tacitly understood that the machine's owners always had first dibs.

Leafy prided himself on consuming only two cups of coffee a day, but his specially selected insulated take-out cup was bigger than most ceremonial Bavarian beer steins and drained approximately half of the contents of an average-sized pot. After completion of the daily barista ritual, the two made their way over to the cubicle that was their designated office area and sat down in their respective chairs.

"Oh man, did I ever have a scary dream last night," said Leafy. "Smelly-Anne Congame and Squirmy Spaniels were facing off in this UFC cage. Associate Justice Brent Hadenough was dressed in this leopard-skin SCOTUS outfit, chugging down beer after beer and pretending to be a blackfaced referee. The darned fight seemed to go on and on forever with both women just pounding away at each other, all limbs a-flying, with no mercy nor quarter. Adam Shiv, Devil Noonez, Linda Greyham and Chuck Schooner were outside hanging onto the side of the cage hurling obscenities at the women and spurring them on to even greater violence. Finally, Spaniels jumps on top of Congame and tries to suffocate her with her breasts . . . and meanwhile, POTUS is out in the audience screaming out to his base about how unfair the whistle-blower laws are and how everybody should read the transcript, while at the same time threatening to send FLOTUS into the cage to even up the odds in the mammary department. And that's when I woke up in a cold sweat, whistling the 'Bridge on the River Kwai' theme and — for some inexplicable reason — in need of a nice, cold drink of milk."

"I wonder how they came up with the term whistle-blower? What about bell-ringer, horn-squeezer, pipe-sucker, string-plucker, drum-banger, ring-dinger . . . ."

"Ring-dinger? Nah."

". . . door-knocker, harp-tweaker, alarm-sounder, wheel-tapper, siren-screamer or even — dare I say it? — blackboard scratcher?"

SNIFF OUT THE LIES

"Whoever *they* are," responded Leafy, "they probably had a very good reason for calling them whistle-blowers . . . with or without the hyphen."

"Definitely without."

"Really? I like it with," opined Leafy. "But in all seriousness, Beefy . . . do you think the President is gonna be impeached?"

"All right. I'll play along with your little game, Leafy . . . but only in the role of the Donald's advocate. First off: There's no evidence of a quid pro quo. And even if there was evidence of a QPQ, there's no real evidence that the President even understands English, never mind Latin. On that basis alone, POTUS is unimpeachable."

"Okay . . . then maybe he's impearable?"

"Nope."

"Implumable?"

"I really don't think so."

"Impruneable?"

"Nah."

"Impapayable?"

"I doubt it."

"Implantainable?"

"Certainly not!"

"Impersimmonable?"

"I'll have to check on that one. I'm pretty sure impersimmonment came up in the Salem witch trials. And you know how witch-hunts play right into the President's all-caps Twitter feed wheelhouse."

"That's a big ten-four. Impineappleable?"

"No way!"

"Impomegranateable?"

"Actually . . . that might be a strong possibility. Subject to a House investigation, he could well be impomegranated. But constitutionally, it would still require a two-thirds majority vote in the Senate."

"Of course, and there lies the rub," affirmed Leafy, with an enigmatic smile.

"But in all seriousness, Leafy. What do you really think is going to come of any half-assed, Trumped-up impeachment proceedings?"

"Exactly what the American people desire the most: commercial-free TV on the major news channels for the duration of the hearings."

"Did you feel those earth tremors last night?" Beefy enquired, abruptly switching the conversational theme from one form of disaster to another.

"Are you kidding me? They damn near shook me out of my bed and I'm pretty sure they were responsible for inducing the Congame-Spaniels nightmare. Somewhere way down deep in the Earth's crust the tension is building, my friend. And you know what? Today could easily be the day of the Big One."

Beefy was originally from Chicago and even after all this time had never quite managed to wrap his mind around the fact that he now lived in an active earthquake zone that was long overdue for a major catastrophe. He had still been living in Illinois when the last substantial seismic event had occurred over two decades ago, but a recent earthquake had registered 7.1 on the Richter scale and it had aroused his latent fears all over again. It had also aroused the latent fears of a whole new generation of Californians. Leafy, on the other hand, was originally from Oakland, and, like most native Californians in his age group, never gave much of a second thought to the occasional rumblings from the ground below. He did, however, experience a perverse joy in fuelling the fires of his Midwestern partner's well-founded fears.

"The San Andreas Fault is only a few miles away," Beefy observed, in an unsuccessful attempt at resigning himself to the inevitable disaster. "I guess if it did happen, there's not too much we could do about it anyway."

"Nada, zip, zero, zilch. There's not a single thing we could do about it, old buddy. USGS says they might be able to give us a ten-second warning, if we're lucky. As far as I'm concerned, that's just about enough time to get under a desk, close your eyes and kiss your family-jewels goodbye. Of course, the same applies to asteroid hits, super-volcanoes, mega-tsunamis, solar mass coronal discharges and the final day of judgement, if that's of any consolation to you."

"Thanks. That actually does make me feel a whole lot better. So what's the plan for today?"

"Catch our killer by lunchtime and spend the rest of the day at the beach sipping ice-cold piña coladas and checking out the scantily clad female volleyball players writhing in the hot sands as they squabble over who exactly it was that dropped the ball."

"That's a good plan and anything's possible . . . but as plans go, that might be just the teensiest bit optimistic."

Armand Hammer had forwarded the enhanced still shot of the athletic Einstein lookalike to the homicide office, which had been duly distributed the night before to patrol units across the city. As of this moment, the BOLO had produced no sightings of the homeless man.

"Let's put the running-man on the back burner, at least for the time being," said Leafy. "I mean, for all we know, he could — at this very moment — be on a freight train bound for Flagstaff, Arizona. If somebody had been chasing me with an AK, I'd either try my very best to stay out of sight or get the hell out of Dodge in a pretty big hurry."

The case was rapidly turning into a whodunit. And while that might be all fine and dandy for the detectives in an Agatha Christie or Conan Doyle story, it was the worst possible scenario for the likes of Leafy Green and Beefy Goodness. The main problem was that there appeared to be no direct causal link between the perpetrator and the victim, and in the real world of investigation, that was how most homicide cases were solved. Yesterday afternoon, officers had canvassed the affluent neighbourhoods that stood at the foot of Mount Lee, but so far none of the residents interviewed had noticed any signs of unusual activity or recognised the picture of the running-man. Regular patrol officers in those areas had informed the detectives that homeless people were now a common sight amongst the homes of the rich and famous and as such, the dispossessed tended to blend into the background. The search for potential witnesses would resume today and there was still hope that some useful nugget of information might yet be discovered.

The forensics lab had examined the spent shell casings for fingerprint and DNA evidence, but the small brass cylinders were as pristine as the day they were shipped from the factory. It was clear that the killer had taken precautions when loading the Kalashnikov rifle's magazine. As of 6:00 PM last night, when the lab had closed, the ejector and firing-pin marks had yielded no connection to any other shooting incidents. The search for a viable comparison would continue when the lab opened for business that morning.

"I know I've said this a million times before," said Beefy, eying Leafy as he guzzled his tankard of sweet, creamy coffee. "But what we need right now is a break."

At that moment, Beefy's desk phone rang. With a hopeful expression on his face, he lifted the receiver.

"Detective Goodness, homicide division . . . No, I don't have any comment right now, except to say that the investigation is proceeding along several avenues of enquiry and that the case has our complete and full attention. Any further enquiries should be routed through the department's public relations office. And one more thing: do *not* call this line again."

The news media, of course, had been all over this case like a pack of wolves on a wounded lamb. This murder contained all the juicy details that Joe Public salivated over and was just the sort of story that increased newspaper sales and TV ratings alike. Like most law- enforcement officers — with the possible exception of police chiefs and their top brass — Leafy and Beefy thought of the media as both an unnecessary distraction and a royal pain in the ass.

"Well," said Leafy, rising to his feet. "I guess there's nothing for it but to go and pound the pavement and talk nicely to the beautiful people."

With the heatwave in full swing and no sign of respite, neither man much relished this particular avenue of enquiry. The adage 'No news is good news' most definitely did not apply to murder investigations and they lingered a few minutes more, hoping one of their phones would ring and deliver that much-needed break in the case; but their communication devices remained stubbornly silent. Leafy topped up his coffee and they headed for the door.

* * *

Despite his lean build and proud Californian heritage, the intense heat affected Leafy far worse than his chunky partner from Illinois. It was now 11:00 AM, and after sweating his butt off on the parched, windy streets of the Hollywood Hills, he had returned to the air-conditioned refuge that was their Crown Victoria. His door-to-door quest had produced no tangible results and he drowned his disappointment in the wave of artificially cooled air that blasted from the dashboard vents while patiently awaiting Beefy's return.

Eventually, he caught sight of Beefy lumbering down a driveway across the street, and he could tell by his partner's body language and the sour expression on his face that he had also struck out on his search for pay dirt. Leafy exited the vehicle and lit up a cigarette as Beefy approached the car.

"This reminds me of my days on patrol," growled Beefy. "All slap and no tickle."

"Don't tell me," said Leafy. "Nobody knows nothing about nothing, and with the property taxes they pay around here, the police should arrest every last one of these filthy homeless bums and drop them off in the desert somewhere between here and Vegas."

"Yeah, that's about the gist of it."

"If we don't pull a rabbit out of the hat pretty soon, old buddy, this case is gonna grow colder than a quarter-pound cheeseburger at a vegan barbecue."

Frustrated, Leafy stomped out his cigarette butt on the pavement. The pair already had two cold cases marring their otherwise unblemished reputation, albeit both in the Crazy category, and the last thing they needed was a third.

"We gotta push the envelope, Leafy."

"We gotta think out of the box."

"We gotta take the bull by the horns."

"We gotta get some skin in the game."

"We gotta sort the wheat from the chaff . . . although I've never really quite understood what that means."

"Well," explained Leafy. "You've got all this wheat in the field, but it's all mixed up with this stuff they call chaff, which is like strips of tin-foil that planes eject to throw enemy missiles off their target . . . ."

Leafy's attention was suddenly diverted to a shapely blonde woman in her mid-thirties, wearing a sky-blue leotard, who was rollerblading down the centre-line of the street with half a dozen dogs on long leashes running behind her. Leafy reacted quickly, flashing his badge and waving her in to the curb.

"Hi there! Sorry to bother you. I'm Detective Green from the Los Angeles Police Department and this is my partner, Detective Goodness. We are investigating a homicide that happened yesterday morning up at the Hollywood Sign."

"Oh yeah. I heard about it on the morning news as I was driving to work. That poor girl. It's so, so sad."

"Yes, it's very sad. Were you in the neighbourhood yesterday morning?"

"You'd better believe it. I run a canine-fitness business," stated the woman, gesturing to the dogs, "and these are some of my furry clients. I'm here every day except weekends — sun, rain, sleet or snow."

She giggled at her little joke, and, by sheer coincidence, Leafy just happened to be extremely partial to good-looking, rollerblading blonde women who liked to giggle at their own silly jokes.

"Funny you should mention snow, because for the last few days I've been dreaming of a white Christmas. That's because I recently won two VIP tickets for a yuletide skiing vacation in Aspen, Colorado. If you don't happen to have any plans firmed up for the Christmas holidays, I'd be honoured to have you join me."

"Tempting as that sounds, Detective Green, I always spend Christmas with my folks. But thanks for the offer."

"You're very welcome. It's just that you have such a peaceful aura surrounding you, I had to give it a shot. I mean, you never know if the boat will float until you drop it in the water. Anyway, what I really need to know is if you noticed anything unusual yesterday morning."

"You're darned right I did!"

Leafy was slightly taken aback at the woman's positive response after all the negativity he and Beefy had encountered in the last few hours. Momentarily, he was lost for words; but he was quick to recover.

"Then I guess my next question is, what *was* the unusual thing you noticed yesterday morning?"

"A black Dodge Charger. It looked like it had just rolled out of the showroom. Tinted windows, mag-alloy wheels, V8 Hemi and all the bells and whistles. It looked like a pretty sweet ride. I drive a completely restored '72 SS Nova, so I know my muscle cars, in case you were wondering."

"What's so unusual about a Dodge Charger? There are lots of them around."

"Not in this neck of the woods, honey. In case you hadn't noticed, we're deep in the heart of Maserati-Ferrari-Bugatti Land. If it doesn't have an 'I' on the end, it's just not worth driving. Nobody around here would be seen dead in a Dodge Charger. It's way too American, if you know what I'm saying."

"Yeah, point taken. So where exactly did you see the Charger?"

"I do a regular morning jogging route with my first batch of doggie clients along the Mulholland Highway from Lake Hollywood Park to the foot of Mount Lee. Near the end of the route the paved highway turns into a dirt road and that's where I saw the Dodge parked off the road between some bushes. That part of the road doesn't have any houses, and it's a dead end. I hardly ever see anybody down there, except for the occasional jogger."

"Did you see anybody in the vehicle?"

"There was nobody inside the car."

"How can you be so sure? You said it had tinted windows."

"Because I walked right up to it and checked out the interior. The rear window wasn't tinted and I could see right inside. And I didn't see anybody around, not even the usual locals."

"Fair enough. I can see that you're a very observant person. So now we get to the sixty-four-thousand-dollar question: did you happen to notice the tag number?"

"You bet I did! It was kind of hard to forget: BADASS 39. I thought it was pretty cool for a vanity plate."

"You just won the grand prize. Unfortunately, I'm a little shy of sixty-four thousand bucks in the bank right now . . . but to show my gratitude, I'd be glad to spring for dinner at any fine restaurant of your choice."

"You just don't give up, do you?"

"Sorry about that. My dad says my inherent stubbornness is a genetic defect from my mother's side of the family. But she claims it's just a mental defect from his side. I think the truth lies somewhere in the middle. Look, before you head off, give me one more chance. Because jogging just happens to be my all-time favourite sport in the whole wide world and dogs just happen to be my all-time favourite animals, maybe one fine morning I could meet you and the doggies down at Lake Hollywood Park in my designer jogging suit and we could all get a little bit of exercise together."

"It's a free country, Detective Green," she responded, with an inscrutable smile. "But you'll have to run pretty fast if you want to keep up with me."

And with that, she was off down the street at a punishing rate of speed, ponytail flying in the breeze and her dogs in tow. Although Leafy was something of a gangly male specimen and really not much to look at, he did surprisingly well when it came to befriending members of the opposite sex.

"I'll take that as a definite maybe."

"Are you *kidding* me?" snorted Beefy through his laughter. "She shot you down three times and you still went back for more. You were starting to sound pretty needy to me, old pal. That was like standing on the same garden rake over and over again and then wondering why you've got this recurring bloody nose."

"Wait a cotton-picking minute now. We can't be talking about the same conversation. All I got was a very positive vibe."

"Just for the record, my long-limbed friend," said Beefy, holding up the fingers of his left hand to count off his observational points with his right. "Number one: you don't have a clue how to ski. Two: you'd sooner have your testicles sawn off with a broken bottle than go jogging. Three: your idea of a fine-dining experience is a Happy Meal in the little kids' section at McDonalds, and lastly but by no means leastly, you've been scared to death of canines ever since that miniature poodle nipped you in the ankle."

"Not all canines. I still like Tucker. And you know full well that poodle was a menace to society. For Christ's sake, Beefy, I had to go have a tetanus shot!"

"You're lucky it didn't have rabies. And that little dog only stood six inches off the ground, was as harmless as a bunny rabbit and you went and stood on its paw. You obviously missed the tactical poodle defence class at the USMC boot camp."

"Now that you come to mention it, I'm fairly certain I was hung-over that day."

"Oh, and by the way. You're slipping up in your old age. In your glory days, you would never have let her go without getting her contact information."

"Call me senile if you want but I'm pretty sure I can find her again if I have to."

"Yeah, maybe so . . . but in the meantime, let's go and find BADASS 39."

* * *

"Bingo!"

Leafy's lanky frame stood hunched over their office PC, left arm braced against the desktop while his right hand tapped out one-fingered commands on the keyboard.

"Rosita Chavez, twenty-four years old. Her current residence is on West Ocean Boulevard, Long Beach. It looks like she moved to California nearly four years ago from Las Cruces, New Mexico. *Oh, looky here!* Rosita must have a few bucks in the bank. Along with the brand-new Charger, she owns a one-year-old Cadillac Escalade, also in black; a three-year-old Hummer H2, black again; and, strangely enough, a four-year-old Dodge Caravan in powder blue."

"Then she's probably got kids," opined Beefy, who sat across from his partner with his feet on the desk, fingers intertwined behind his head and his eyes peacefully closed. "The Caravan may not be the sportiest vehicle on the market, but it's had a five-star safety rating for the last seven years in a row. My sister's got one and all she thinks about in life are her kids and how to keep them safe. Has our Ms. Chavez got any criminal history?"

With a few clicks of the mouse, Leafy transitioned from the DMV site to the National Criminal Database.

"Nothing recent. She's got one juvenile offence at the age of sixteen, but the court records are sealed. She did three months' probation, no fine and no time served. Is it worth the aggravation to try to get the records unsealed?"

"The courts are pretty tight-lipped when it comes to juvie stuff. And with a slap on the wrist like that it couldn't have been very serious . . . and definitely not violent. I'm guessing shoplifting or something related to school. Let's move on to the social media search. That's usually where we strike the motherlode when everything else fails."

"Here we go," said Leafy, as he moved to the new search engine. "Good, old Fakebook: the gift that just keeps on giving. When will these dumb-ass criminals ever realize that after cell phones, social media is their worst enemy?"

"Hopefully never. Otherwise, I wouldn't be able to sit here relaxing on my big, fat ass listening to you tell me all about their Fakebook pages."

"Well, you were right on the money with the kids. 'Rosie' has a boy and a girl aged two and three: Carlos and Gabriela. She still stays in contact with her family back in Las Cruces. She's a Catholic — surprise, surprise — and, according to her profile, she still goes to church."

"I was brought up a Catholic, and believe me, they make it very tough to cancel your subscription. You gotta keep clicking and clicking as hard as you can on that unsubscribe button for days on end until finally an avatar of *Il Papa* pops up on the screen and whispers: 'Okay my son, you're good to go.'"

"As a non-practising Jewish person, I'm really glad you shared that with me. If we want out of the faith, we just stop going to the synagogue . . . but getting back to Ms Chavez: her mom works as a cook in a high-school cafeteria in Las Cruces and her dad is a long-haul truck driver. Her family is not exactly at the top of the financial food chain, if you catch my drift. I wonder how Rosie managed to get so wealthy so quickly."

"Maybe she's got some marketable skills that haven't as yet come to light. Try the picture gallery. One good picture, if it's painted just right, might save us a thousand words."

"And here she is, standing proudly beside BADASS 39. It has to be said, that's a very nice-looking chassis . . . and the car's not too shabby either."

Interest piqued, Beefy raised himself from the chair and peered over Leafy's shoulder. The picture showed Chavez in a pair of cut-off jean shorts, a pink tank-top and a pair of pink high-heel shoes. Even with the heels, she was not very tall, but her body was perfectly proportioned and her carefully made-up face, framed by curly, lustrous black hair, was the epitome of classic Latino beauty.

"I think we just found her marketable skills," remarked Leafy, as he scrolled down through the images.

"And who do we have here?" asked Beefy.

"I'm thinking that's the babies' daddy. The caption reads: 'Me, Jesús and the kids enjoying a day on the beach.' Now Beefy, that's a face that you'd *never* get tired of kicking."

The picture showed Rosita and the two toddlers sitting beside a half-constructed sandcastle, their faces clearly reflecting the simple happiness of the moment. Above them towered the hulking figure of a hard-core Hispanic gangbanger, with the mandatory long, baggy shorts, an immaculately white T-shirt and a pair of loosely laced basketball shoes that probably cost more than a homicide detective made in a month. His head was shaved bald and every inch of exposed skin on his body was covered in gangland tattoos. Especially menacing was the fact that he had also waxed off his natural eyebrows so as not to conflict with the sloping, Devil's eyebrows tattooed above his cold, dark eyes. Even on a family outing, it looked like Rosita's baby-daddy was still taking care of business, with a phone pinned to his ear while he attempted to smile happily for the camera. The attempt was a complete failure and it only served to make his face look even scarier and more evil than if he'd left it in neutral mode.

"Talk about Beauty and the Beast," said Leafy. "I'll bet Jesús is a big hit at the Chavez family reunions."

"That's one scary-looking dude, all right. This boy is totally committed to the 'Life' and there'll be no going back to the civilian world for him. He might be living high on the hog right now, but sooner or later — and probably sooner — he's gonna end up like all of these animals do: caged up for life or a bullet-ridden corpse. Do me a favour. Zoom in on that tattoo on his neck. I don't recall seeing that one before."

Before transferring to Homicide, Beefy had a done a two-year stint in the Gang Unit, and while he was not up on the latest and greatest in the world of gangstas, he was familiar with most of their traditional insignia. Leafy focussed the view onto the gangbanger's thickly muscled neck. The tattoo was in the shape of an unfurled scroll with the letters ESBSB imprinted upon it. Compared to Malverde's other tattoos — which were of a high professional quality — both the letters and the scroll had been crudely inscribed and displayed all of the hallmarks of a jailhouse tattoo.

"That's a new one on me," declared Beefy, as he jotted down the series of letters in his notebook. "Let's get a printout on the beach photo and maybe we'll slide over and have a little chat with the good people at the Gang Unit."

"You don't really need me to come along, do you?" asked Leafy, grimacing as if he had just swallowed something extremely sour.

"We've all got to face our demons, old chum. And who knows? Maybe Irma won't even be there."

* * *

Lieutenant Irma Manstein was the boss of the Gang Unit, and at six-foot-six and nearly thirty inches wide, she cut a most imposing figure. The unit's unofficial motto read: 'Dress how you like, just don't get killed' and Manstein fully subscribed to that credo. Today, she was decked out in loose-fitting battle fatigues, with an old-school, nickel-plated Colt 45 semi-automatic holstered at her side, gunfighter style. She was definitely not the sort of girl you would want to have knocking at your door at five in the morning, let alone kicking it down. The two homicide detectives almost felt sorry for any gang members unfortunate enough to cross paths with the Gang Unit's supreme commander.

"Hey, Beefy!" exclaimed Manstein as she caught sight of her old partner in crime- reduction. "You big old dog, how are they hanging?"

"They're hanging lower and lower with each year that passes, Irma. How about you?"

"Mine are hanging pretty high. And that's just the way I like them. I see you've still got your marine sidekick dangling off your shirttails. That's too bad."

Leafy and Irma had never hit it off; for whatever reason she just loathed the sight of him, and he was scared to death of her.

"Hi, Irma," injected Leafy. "Please don't beat me up. I really am one of the good guys, you know."

Manstein was an army veteran and a martial-arts instructor, and in her younger, wilder days had indeed beaten up many a drunken Navy boy who had been stupid enough to mouth off in her presence. Irma cupped a meaty hand around her ear.

"Did you hear something, Beefy? It sounded like a mouse or some other kind of vermin. Damn it! That means I'm gonna have to call in the exterminators."

"Settle down, girl," soothed Beefy, "or he'll be pouting for the rest of the day."

Beefy handed the Facebook picture to her and silently awaited her response.

"The girl is a little cutie pie," she observed with a suggestive smile. "Too bad she's hooked up with a piece of crap like that."

Manstein was a proud and unapologetic lesbian and she flaunted her sexual preferences to anyone within earshot or eyeshot. She had never had to come out of the closet, because she had not been aware the closet even existed.

"Do you happen to know this particular piece of crap's name?" probed Beefy.

"Jesús Malverde . . . also known as El Carnicero."

"The Butcher," Beefy translated. "For some reason or other, that name really seems to suit him."

"You bet it does. A few years back, before his star had risen in LA, he worked freelance for the cartels as an enforcer on the Mexican border. They say he had a collection of over a thousand human ears, a strong testament to his skill with a machete. Who did he kill this time?"

"We suspect he may have some connection to the Hollywood Sign case."

"Really?" asked Manstein, genuinely surprised. "Killing cheesecake fashion models is not exactly in his wheelhouse. This boy is all about business, and these days he tends to limit his savagery to competing gangbangers trying to muscle in on his action."

"And what kind of action is that?"

"Premium-grade Asian heroin at bargain-basement prices. That's his little niche in the market."

"Oh yeah, I heard heroin had suddenly come back in fashion. It almost makes you yearn for the good old cocaine days. I guess the Taliban have families to feed, just like everyone else. Tell me something, Irma. What do the letters ESBSB stand for? I assume they are initials of some kind?"

"The East Side Barrio Scum Boyz."

"The East Side Barrio Scum Boyz. You're kidding me, right?"

"You've been out of the Gang Unit for a long time, Beefy. It's not just the Crips, the Bloods and the Sureños anymore. ESBSB is an offshoot of MS 13. Apparently they were going to call themselves MS 14.5, but somehow that never really caught on."

"For pity's sake, Irma, surely they could have come up with a snappier name than the East Side Barrio Scum Boyz?"

"It's just like band names, Beefy. All the good ones are already taken. Black Oak Arkansas, Led Zeppelin, The Kentucky Head-hunters, The

Fabulous Thunderbirds, Nirvana . . . those are all names that a girl can really get her teeth into. Now look what we've got: The Sheepdogs and The Black Eyed Peas. *Good grief!* Where did all the creativity go?"

"It's the same with TV shows, Irma," replied Beefy, warming to the theme. "No originality whatsoever. Remakes of Magnum PI, MacGyver and Hawaii Five-O, for God's sake. Not to mention Baywatch remastered!"

Beefy and Irma laughed just like old times and Leafy stood back, wisely staying out of reach of Manstein's long arms of the law. Manstein's voice suddenly became low and conspiratorial, and she looked around the office to see if anybody was within earshot.

"Listen, Beefy, I guess I'd better level with you. But this is highly classified information and you didn't hear it from me. Okay?"

"Okay."

"And that goes for your skinny sidekick as well."

"Okay," Leafy affirmed obediently.

"For the last three years, my unit has been working alongside the DEA and the FBI on a big undercover operation that could take down hundreds of bad guys from all across the US and beyond. Malverde is one of the mid-level players we've been waiting to take down, but we have to hang in there until there's enough evidence in the bag to get at the real movers and shakers."

"If Malverde is our killer," inserted Beefy in a very serious tone. "And I'll be right up front with you, Irma, we don't have a shred of evidence to support that theory — then big undercover operation or not, if he turns out to be our guy we're gonna slap the cuffs on him."

"I don't think so, Beefy," replied Manstein, with a humourless smirk. "Immigration and Customs Enforcement picked him up two hours ago and Malverde is currently cooling his heels in an ICE detention centre, no pun intended. I just had a blistering row with them on the phone. We had an arrangement in place with ICE for them to leave Malverde and a few of the key local players alone until our investigation was completed.

And now they've gone and stabbed us in the back. The bottom line is that ICE wants to deport him back to El Salvador but we want to strap him to a gurney and shove a big, fat needle in his arm. The whole thing is turning into a complete fuck-up and I'm so mad I could kick the shit out of half a dozen marines."

"Easy now, Irma. Did the ICE people tell you why they messed up and jumped the gun?"

"Apparently, they didn't mess up. That surly prick of an ICE agent told me that the order to detain Malverde 'came straight from the top', whatever the hell that means."

A distinct feeling of unease enveloped the two homicide detectives as they realized that their main suspect in N. Emma Johnson's murder might well be out of reach and that there could be a lot more to this case than at first met the eye.

* * *

Having consumed a quick drive-thru lunch, Leafy and Beefy sat quietly in their parked vehicle pondering the case and contemplating what their next move should be. Thirty hours had elapsed since their victim had been gunned down, and with every passing minute the evidentiary scent trail grew ever fainter. Their only viable suspect — and this was, at best, only an educated hunch — was now in federal legal limbo awaiting his deportation hearing, and without hard evidence that connected him to the murder, that is where he would stay until Uncle Sam saw fit to send him back to El Salvador. To compound an already complicated situation, Malverde was also one of several subjects being scrutinized in a completely separate investigation involving federal and local law-enforcement agencies, all of whom would dearly love to get their hands on him just as much as the two homicide detectives. After research-ing the gangbanger, it was fairly obvious that Malverde had taken the precaution of placing all his material and financial assets into his lady friend's name to prevent future seizure by the authorities as the profits of his criminal activities. This meant there was no direct link between him and the vehicle seen parked at the foot of Mount Lee around the time of the murder.

With a loud and disgusting noise, Leafy sucked out the remnants of his super-sized strawberry shake and then crumpled the empty container into his take-out bag.

"Putting theories aside for a minute, what do we know for sure?"

"Not too much," replied Beefy, still sipping on his bottle of pure mountain-spring water. "Our victim was inadvertently killed during the commission of another crime. The weapon used was almost certainly an AK-47. The intended victim appears to be an urban outdoorsman who, despite his advanced age, seems to be as swift and sure-footed as a goddamned mountain goat. A gangsta bling-mobile was spotted in the vicinity of the crime scene, which belongs — at least officially — to a young mother of two who has known ties to a local mid-level drug lord. The day after our murder, the aforementioned drug lord is arrested by ICE despite a prior arrangement with other agencies not to do so. That's all I got at this particular moment."

"Okay," responded Leafy, as he tried to think things through. "Ignoring Malverde's detention for the time being, it seems to me it all boils down to three things: recovery of the weapon, finding the intended victim and a forensic examination of BADASS 39."

"Short of releasing the running-man's picture to the media and giving him his fifteen minutes of fame, there's not much more we can do to locate him. But that course of action could easily backfire on us and send him scurrying even deeper into the woods. We should save that as a last resort."

"Roger that. That leaves us with the weapon and the car. Finding the car shouldn't be much of a problem, but what are the chances that the AK is still around?"

"If it was you or me who committed this murder, Leafy, that rifle would by now be dismantled and the pieces deposited in several locations at the bottom of the Pacific Ocean. But we're talking *gangbangers* here, and you know how attached they can get to their automatic long guns. Even if he was smart enough to get rid of it, maybe the ICE guys grabbed him before he could do it."

As a general rule of thumb, illegal handguns were quite easy to obtain on the streets of LA if a person knew the right places to look. Lower-quality burners — weapons that had been used in previous crimes — could be purchased for as little as fifty bucks and a clean, halfway decent name-brand pistol fetched an average price of around $350 on the streets. This was not exactly a huge investment for the criminals when one considered the immense tax-free profits that could be garnered from the sale of narcotics or armed robbery. Consequently, most criminals had no qualms about ditching a handgun that they had fired during the commission of a crime and simply replacing it with another one.

Illegal fully automatic weapons, however, were in an entirely different league to their smaller cousins. From sexy little Uzis and Tech Nines to large-calibre, belt-fed military machine guns — and indeed, everything in between — automatic weapons were available to criminals, but at a much higher price tag than handguns. In addition, their procurement required knowledge of the specialized underworld dealers who sold such weapons and, as such, usually ended up in the hands of full-time career criminals with deep pockets.

There was also the psychological aspect to consider, and this was especially true of gang-affiliated drug-dealer types. Their whole world was based on one single premise: the acquisition of raw power. The power to control a street corner, a neighbourhood or even a whole city, and nothing screamed power louder than a hand-held device that sprayed high-velocity chunks of hot metal at anyone who dared to challenge their authority. As a result, many of these criminals came to love and cherish their automatic instruments of destruction and were oftentimes loath to ever part with them. For law-enforcement personnel this was a double-edged sword. On the one hand, they faced death or crippling injuries at the business end of these weapons, and on the other, the forensic opportunity to connect the owners of the guns with their previous acts of violence.

"Malverde's not going anywhere anytime soon," opined Leafy. "But Rosita might well be a different story. If you put yourself in her position, she's just lost her big, bad boyfriend, she's living in a city a long way from home, she probably hasn't made that many friends in LA and she has the welfare of her kids to consider. She may also be afraid that the cops are going to come knocking on her door and lock her sweet little ass up in jail. It makes you wonder what Rosie's next move is gonna to be."

"It wouldn't be beyond the bounds of possibility that she might pack up the kids and high-tail it back to Mommy and Daddy in Las Cruces. I'm gonna call the office and get some squad cars over there pronto to make sure she doesn't skedaddle."

"We don't have enough probable cause for a search warrant," observed Leafy. "The worst thing we can charge her with is a parking viola-tion . . . and even that's a little iffy."

"That's very true," replied Beefy, with a sneaky smile. "But I'm pretty sure Rosie doesn't know that. When she sees the uniforms arrive at her door with Family Services in tow to take her children into protective custody, then who knows? Maybe we can convince her that it's in her best interests to consent to a search of her property."

* * *

By the time the uniformed officers arrived at her Long Beach home, Rosita Chavez and her two children had already flown the coop. Of the four vehicles registered to her name, the blue Dodge Caravan was missing and a state-wide All Points Bulletin had been issued on the vehicle. Within the space of two hours, Chavez had been apprehended and she had been summarily returned to Los Angeles to be interviewed at the homicide office. The children were now in the temporary care of Family Services and Rosita sat alone in one of the unit's windowless interrogation rooms looking forlorn, yet proudly defiant. No weapons or incriminating evidence had been found in her van.

Leafy and Beefy had been watching her on the video monitor for the last ten minutes as she fidgeted and squirmed on the uncomfortable seat, displaying all the customary signs of nervousness associated with an impending interview with homicide detectives. It was fairly obvious to both men that while she was associated with a serious criminal, she was not one herself.

"I read online that they're thinking of getting rid of the SATs as a prerequisite for college admissions," said Beefy, apropos of nothing and killing just a little more time.

"Oh yeah? Well that's fine by me. If I'd only known that you could just bribe your way into college, I probably wouldn't be sitting here talking to you about college admissions tests right now."

"So where would you be?"

"In jail for accepting college admissions bribes. I saw this one SAT practise question and it went something like: If the Three Amigos, the Squad, the Gang of Four, the Magnificent Seven, Ocean's Thirteen and the entire cast of 'Hamilton' were all queuing up outside a gender-neutral public washroom somewhere Off Broadway and six actors and two politicians in the queue got tired of waiting and urinated outside against the wall and/or onto the pavement, how many people subsequently relieved themselves in the washroom's legally-sanctioned toilet bowls? Besides being equipped with eight cubicles, the washroom also contained three urinals of which only two were functional."

"That's a toughie. So what was the answer?"

"Minus seven hundred and forty-two point four."

"That's gotta be a trick question," objected Beefy, "I got minus seven hundred and forty-one point eight."

"The SATs are all trick questions. Here's another one: If you lived in the Bronx in the mid-nineteen eighties, owned a three-year-old Buick LeSabre with a highway gas consumption of fifteen miles to the gallon and ate bacon and eggs for breakfast on every day of the year except Thanksgiving, what would you have called an under-depilated mob-boss's wife?"

When Beefy failed to respond to his partner's alleged SAT conundrum, Leafy gratuitously provided the answer.

"A furry godmother."

"Hmm . . . has Rosita stewed long enough?" asked Beefy.

"Yeah. I think she's just about ready," replied Leafy. "There's nothing worse than an overcooked witness."

"What do you say we go in there and sniff out the lies?"

"Copy that."

Leafy unlocked the interrogation room door, with lots of rattling of keys and clicking of locks, just to make sure Rosita fully understood the gravity of her situation and that her freedom was very much at stake. It had been agreed that Beefy would conduct the first part of the interview, and the two detectives and another officer entered the room.

The detectives sat down at the table and Beefy commenced the proceedings.

"Rosita Chavez?"

"Yes," she answered.

"I'm Detective Goodness and this is Detective Green . . . and this little, four-legged fella is K9 Officer Tucker. You don't mind us having a dog present for this interview, do you?"

Rosita looked slightly taken aback by the presence of the dog, but Tucker was a small cocker-poo with a friendly demeanour and a cute reflective-orange K9 vest strapped to his back. He was not a young dog and he had wise, intelligent eyes. Rosita merely shrugged in acceptance. Beefy unclipped Tucker's leash. Unprompted, the dog went and sat in the far corner of the room, facing the people and paying close attention to the proceedings.

"Ms. Chavez, we want to talk to you about a murder that happened yesterday morning in the vicinity of the Hollywood Sign. Did you happen to hear about it on the news?"

"Yeah, I heard about it. What's that got to do with me?"

"We'll get to that, Ms. Chavez. Right now, I'll bet you're worried about your kids. I just want to put your mind at rest and let you know that they are perfectly safe in the custody of Family Services. And no matter what the outcome of this interview, I guarantee they will be well taken care of."

"Why should I be worried about my kids? I haven't done anything wrong."

As the last word came out of her mouth, Tucker let out a single, unaggressive bark. Rosita was startled by the sudden percussive sound and Leafy silently jotted something down in his notebook.

"We'll come back to that statement in a minute," said Beefy, pressing on. "You own several automobiles, Ms. Chavez. We are specifically interested in your black Dodge Charger with the vanity plate: B-A-D-A-S-S 39."

Beefy deliberately spelled out the letters on the vehicle tag as opposed to pronouncing them as a word. He waited a moment to let that information sink in and then resumed the interview.

"Witnesses have confirmed that it was parked on the Mulholland Highway yesterday morning in the vicinity of Mount Lee around the time of the murder. Is there any good reason why it was parked in that area at that time?"

Rosita remained silent.

"Were you driving the Charger yesterday morning?"

"No."

"Then who was driving it?"

"I have no idea who was driving it."

Tucker gave another single bark and Leafy made another entry in his notebook.

"All right, Ms. Chavez. Let's approach this from a different angle. Who, besides yourself, has access to or permission to drive your Dodge Charger?"

"It's usually parked out on the street and anybody could have taken it on that day."

In general, Beefy was not an aggressive interrogator. He preferred a softer approach, taking his time while allowing the subjects to see the errors in their own logic. His calm, non-confrontational style usually paid dividends and he allowed a short period of complete silence to elapse before underscoring the fallacious absurdity of her statement.

"Ms. Chavez, if you're suggesting that your Charger was stolen, then why would a thief return it to exactly the same place it was stolen from? That doesn't make a lick of sense."

Again, Rosita remained stubbornly silent.

"All right, Ms. Chavez," said Beefy, with a disappointed shake of his head. "At this point in the interview I'm going to have to hand you over to Detective Green here."

Leafy's style of interrogation could best be described as highly unpredictable. He rolled his chair in closer to the interviewee and offered her a disarming smile.

"Ms. Chavez," began Leafy. "Do you mind if I call you Rosita?"

Rosita gave an indifferent shrug.

"Rosita . . . let me explain our situation to you. After that, we'll see how our situation compares with your situation. If everything is copacetic and both situations jive together, then you and Carlos and Gabriela can be on your way, free to go about your business. All I want is for you to tell the *truth*. Is that too much to ask?"

"Okay," replied Rosita.

"Great! Now I think we're getting somewhere. Is Jesús Malverde the father of your children?"

"Yes."

"And in point of fact, it was Jesús who paid for all the cars and the house and everything else?"

"No . . . ."

Tucker sounded his restrained bark and Beefy quietly commended the dog with a doggie treat and made an entry in his notebook.

"Now, Rosita, what did I just say about telling the truth? You do realize who we are, don't you? We're the Death Police."

"The Undertaker Squad," put in Beefy.

"The Reaper Unit," returned Leafy.

"The Rest in Peace and May God Have Mercy on Your Soul Cops," said Beefy.

"We are the *Big League*. Maybe this would be no big deal for a tough guy like Jesús, but are you really ready for the Big League, Rosita? I don't think you are. You are telling outright lies to homicide detectives. Do you know what that's called? That's called hindering the course of an investigation. That's called three to seven years hard time in San Quentin. What about the kids? They won't go to their grandparents in Las Cruces. Oh *hell* no. They'll be assigned as wards of the court and a judge will decide where they will end up. It could be anywhere. A state institution, fostered out to needy parents, some crazy religious cult . . . who the hell knows? This is California for Christ's sake! Anything could happen to them without their mom around. And even if you survive a maximum-security prison term — and there's no real guarantee you will — you'll have to fight in the courts to try to get the kids back. And believe me, Rosita, family court judges are not usually too happy about returning children to convicted felons, and child-custody lawyers can cost a ton of bucks. Think about what I'm saying, girl. Or at the very least, think of your kids."

"I swear I'm not telling any lies!"

Tucker barked yet again, and this time Rosita's thin veneer of indifference finally broke down.

"What is it with that *stupid, freaking dog*? Why does it keep barking like that?"

"K9 Officer Tucker is anything but stupid, Rosita," Leafy explained in a patient voice. "In fact, he's a very smart dog. But that's not where his real talents lie. His real talent lies in his nose and his ability to detect minute scent particles in the air around him."

"Okay," replied Rosita, "So he's a sniffer dog, so what?"

"Things have come a long way since the old days when dogs were used mainly for tracking down escaped prisoners. These days, K9s are used to detect narcotics, explosives, cadavers, radioactive materials and various other biological and chemical substances. If something has a scent — and I'm reliably informed that just about everything does — then a dog can be trained to sniff it out. Are you with me so far, Rosita?"

"I'm not stupid. I get it. Everyone knows that dogs are good at sniffing things out."

"That's right. And Tucker here is especially good at sniffing a person's body odour. I don't know the ins and outs of the whole thing, but apparently a person's body odour is like a cocktail . . . and just like a tequila sunrise, the 'taste' of this cocktail can vary from minute to minute, depending on the circumstances and the ingredients used to concoct it. It's all about these things called pheromones."

"All right, thanks for the science lesson. But what's all that got to do with the price of beef in Texas?"

"*Really*, Rosita?" protested Leafy, his tone both scathing and impatient. "You're still giving me the attitude? You seem pretty sharp to me. Do I have to lay it out for you? All right, I'll give you a clue: Rosita's father is a chartered accountant from Phoenix, Arizona."

Tucker barked as soon as Leafy finished the statement.

"Now, check this out: Rosita's father is a truck driver from Las Cruces, New Mexico."

The dog remained silent.

"Rosita's mother is an exotic dancer in a New Orleans nightclub," Beefy chimed in.

The dog barked.

"Rosita's mother works in a high-school cafeteria in Las Cruces," corrected Leafy.

Canine silence greeted the remark.

The two detectives watched in amused silence as Rosita struggled to wrap her mind around what was happening. Finally, she hesitantly managed to voice her thoughts.

"He's . . . a *lie*-sniffing dog?"

"Way to go, Rosita!" said Leafy, clapping his hands together. The two men applauded her answer as though encouraging the progress of a slow student.

"Tucker boy here is about 97 percent accurate. That's way better than a standard polygraph."

"That's way better than God," Beefy quipped.

"I don't believe you," said Rosita, still trying to maintain some semblance of defiance in a world that had been turned upside down.

Sensing that the time was right, Leafy stood up and withdrew a pair of handcuffs from his belt.

"Believe what you want, Rosie. But if you don't start playing ball right now, I guarantee you'll be wearing orange coveralls tonight while the jailhouse butch queens fight each other for a piece of your pretty little ass."

Beefy laid a calming hand on his partner's arm and Leafy withdrew to Tucker's corner.

"Rosita," said Beefy, with a sad smile. "You must have known this day would be coming sooner or later. You've spent three years with a two-legged death machine called Jesús Malverde and now you've got to face up to it, girl: the good times are over. The only thing you can do right now is to try to minimise the damage to yourself . . . and to your kids."

Rosita put her hands to her face. Silently she wept, her shoulders heaving under the huge emotional weight that pressed down upon her. Leafy glanced at his partner with a triumphant grin and gave a thumbs-up gesture lauding his Oscar-winning performance. At last, Rosita spoke up in a tone of abject defeat.

"What do you want to know?"

"First off," said Leafy. "We need your consent to search the Long Beach property and all the vehicles."

"Okay, you have my consent."

"Secondly," said Beefy. "We need to know where Jesús put the AK-47."

"Jesús has lots of guns and most of them are still in the house. Some of his friends were going to come over tonight and clear them out."

"Where's the AK-47?"

"He called me from the detention centre and told me to get rid of the chopper."

Chopper was street-speak for an automatic assault rifle.

"Where did you get rid of it?" Beefy pressed.

"I threw it down a storm drain over on the LA River by the Metro rail yards. I can show you where it is."

* * *

Vasquez had taken the detectives to the place where she had dumped the gun. She was now back at headquarters, temporarily housed with her children in one of the upper-floor conference rooms until the search teams had concluded their business. Her fate was in the hands of the district attorney and Leafy and Beefy had moved on to assist in the search of her Long Beach home.

'K9 Officer' Tucker and the ultrasonic signalling device that had come along with him had been duly returned to the movie animal trainer to whom they belonged. This was Tucker's third interrogation with Leafy and Beefy, and in each one important information had been gleaned from the subject. Subterfuge, trickery and even outright lying were all legally acceptable methods of eliciting truthful information during a police interview. Whether or not such information had any evidentiary value in a court of law was a question for the judges and lawyers to work out.

But just like polygraphs, sting operations or even the use of psychics, for that matter, information derived may or may not be viewed as hard evidence, but it could be used to move forward on a stagnant investigation by creating fresh leads, probable cause or consent for a search. Leafy and Beefy employed the lie-sniffing routine sparingly because it was only applicable if the circumstances were just right. Although the Department grudgingly condoned its use, they flatly refused to finance the canine ploy. Fortunately, the animal trainer was an ex-LAPD K9 officer and he charged Leafy and Beefy only a minimal fee to cover his expenses.

For the lie-sniffing ruse to work successfully, three factors had to be right. Firstly, the interrogators must have some indisputable facts at their disposal and a viable theory of the subject's knowledge of the crime. Secondly, the subject must be amenable to the concept, and this did not necessarily mean they were gullible or stupid. The incredible acuity of a canine's olfactory sense was common knowledge and scientifically proven beyond doubt; so it was only a tiny leap of faith for a well-selected subject to buy into the plausibility of the idea. And lastly, to avoid even the appearance of coercion, the dog itself must not appear intimidating, and macho breeds such as Dobermans and German Shepherds were completely out of the question. The cuter the better, and Tucker had been specifically chosen with this in mind. Tucker was not only a gifted actor, but he could sit motionless for hours on end, dutifully barking each time the concealed ultrasonic command device button was pressed. The whole scenario was akin to the illusion created in a well-orchestrated conjuror's trick.

It was also a heck of a lot of fun.

CHAPTER FOUR

A Whore's Panties

Beefy slowed the Crown Victoria to fifty as he made the wide, sweeping turn from I-210 onto Interstate 15, heading up into the foothills of the Sierras towards the town of Victorville. A few miles north of Victorville was their destination, the Adelanto Detention Facility, a USCIS administered prison complex run by Immigration and Customs Enforcement officers. Leafy and Beefy had visited Adelanto on a couple of prior occasions, and on a light traffic day such as today, the journey from downtown LA could be made in as little as ninety minutes.

It was nine in the morning on the third day of the N. Emma Johnson case, and things seemed to be shaping up quite nicely. The AK-47 had been recovered from the storm drain and was undergoing examination at the forensics lab. The same scrutiny was being applied to the Dodge Charger BADASS 39. Leafy, Beefy and a team of other officers had scoured Rosita's Long Beach home and surrounding property, but apart from finding an illegal handgun in each room of the sixteen-room house, the place had been spic and span and devoid of any other illegal items. Two laptop computers, an Android tablet and four cell phones had been seized and duly dispatched to the Digital Forensics Unit. Armand

Hammer had just called Beefy to let him know that those items would receive priority treatment and an examination report would be ready by the end of the day.

An interview with their only suspect, Jesús Malverde, had been booked for ten o'clock this morning and with about forty-five miles still left of their journey, that timeline was easily attainable. For once, both detectives were well rested and had a solid plan of attack in place, and the higher they climbed into the mountains the cooler and clearer the air became. Despite the grimness of their destination and the fact that they would soon be in close proximity to a truly evil human being, it felt good to escape the stiflingly hot streets of Los Angeles, if only for a few hours.

Beefy set the cruise control to fifty-four miles per hour and lifted his foot from the gas pedal. The two had been largely silent on this trip; a comfortable, contemplative silence that merely indicated that neither man had anything much to say. Eventually, Leafy chose to break that silence.

"I don't *get* dancing."

"Dancing?"

"Yeah, dancing. I just don't get it."

"What's not to get about dancing? You move your body to the rhythm of the music. That's all there is to it. What don't you get about that?"

"It's the whole concept. I mean, where did people ever come up with the idea of dancing? I would never have come up with the idea of dancing on my own. It serves no real purpose. It doesn't provide humans with any evolutionary advantage in the fight for survival. If anything, it's an impediment to survival. It's like, while you and your tribe are strutting your stuff outside the communal cave, the bad-guy tribe from across the mountain sneaks up and rapes the men and pillages the women. And have you ever really watched people when they're dancing? It's a ridiculous way to pass the time. People look silly when they dance. I look silly when I dance. Even top-notch professional dancers look silly when they dance. Am I the only one who sees it like this?"

"Well, first off, Leafy, you're a white boy . . . ."

"That's downright racist!"

"... and nobody really expects white boys to do too much in the dancing department. Just like basketball. There are a few exceptions — like Shawn Spicey for instance — but by and large white boys are what we in the dancing world like to call choreographically challenged. It's just like being born blind or deaf or stupid. It's a handicap ... and it's very, very sad. Just get on with your life, man, and concentrate on all the good things and try not to dwell on your disability."

"Do you know, Beefy? I think I'm feeling better about it already. I'm really glad we had this conversation."

"Me too."

They relapsed into a comfortable, contemplative silence. Eventually, Leafy chose to break that silence.

"What do you do with your arms when you're asleep?"

"I really wouldn't know. You wanna know why? Because I'm asleep."

"All right, I'll rephrase that. What do you do with your arms just *before* you go to sleep?"

Beefy gave the question some considerable consideration, picturing himself beside his wife in their king-sized bed in the moments before unconsciousness.

"I don't do anything with my arms before I go to sleep. They just hang in there, free to do whatever they want to do until I wake up the next morning."

"So you've got this kind of unwritten contract with your arms," observed Leafy. "That when you're asleep, they can goof off and flail around the bed all they want, as long as they're available for whatever you need them for when you wake up."

"You better believe it. I've got the same deal going with my head, my legs, my torso and my penis."

"So you're telling me that your penis has the full run of the house when you're asleep? And when you wake up, you have no idea where it's been or what it's been up to?"

"That's right," replied Beefy proudly. "But I know the old John Thomas can't roam too far because it's securely attached to that very large mass of flesh, bone, sinew and gristle called William Goodness, who in turn is guarded by his very light-sleeping wife. There was a time when my penis might have thought about gaining some sort of nocturnal freedom, but that was all just a crazy dream. So do you have some sort of problem with your arms when you're sleeping? What do you do with your arms before you go to sleep?"

"I don't do nothing with my arms. My arms are just fine when I'm sleeping."

Beefy momentarily took his eyes off the freeway and offered his partner a sideways glance.

"You truly are a facile person," he observed. "Do you ever give any thought to the serious issues of the day? To any of the burning political questions that are facing America at this very moment?"

"Sure I do."

"Like what?"

"Well . . . if POTUS and FLOTUS went riding in a Lotus, would SCOTUS even notice?"

"Jesus H. Christ!" replied Beefy, amused and appalled but by no means surprised. "Leafy, you must have realized at this stage in your life that your elevator doesn't quite reach the top floor. And of course, you were never exactly the brightest bulb in the chandelier, were you?"

"Hey, that's a serious political question."

"Okay. So what's the serious answer to your serious political question?"

"SCOTUS wouldn't notice, but the voters at General Motors would almost certainly notice POTUS and FLOTUS riding in a Lotus."

"Please don't take this the wrong way," said Beefy. "But you're a god-damned idiot."

"Right back at you, muchacho."

For the first time in several weeks, Beefy switched off the vehicle's air conditioner, and yet again, the two lapsed into a comfortable, contemplative silence. This time Beefy broke that silence.

"I was waiting in line at the bank the other day, and I saw that TV inventor guy behind me in the queue. I can't recall his name ... but do you remember those commercials about relieving stiffness and sore backs while you're driving in your car?"

"Driva-Bubble, Driva-Bubble," sung Leafy, who never let the fact that he couldn't hold a tune to save his life deter him from singing with verve and conviction, "alleviates your spinal trouble."

"Precisely," affirmed Beefy. "He's the one who came up with the original idea of cutting a hole in your vehicle's roof and fitting a Plexiglas dome so you can stand up while you're driving. Apparently, the optional treadmill attachment was his wife's idea."

"You see, Beefy, ideas like that are what's going to Make America Great Again."

"Damn straight they are! It's just like that recumbent exercise couch with the built-in TV and soda pop dispenser that my wife got me for our anniversary."

Coincidentally, a blood-red Bugatti Vayron II overtook them at a high rate of speed with a Driva-Bubble fitted to both the driver and passenger sides of its roof.

"Wasn't that David McSavage driving that? The boss of that brainwashing, pseudo-scientific, anti-psychiatry, holy-roller cult over on Sunset Boulevard," queried Leafy.

"David *Miscarriage*," corrected Beefy. "Yeah, as a matter of fact, I think it was."

"It looked like he was punching somebody out in the Driva-Bubble next to him."

"That's okay ... as long as it was for purely religious reasons."

"First Amendment rights? Right?"

"You better believe it," asserted Beefy, knowledgably. "You're free to beat up whoever you want to beat up in this country, as long as it's in the name of the Judeo-Christian-God or some other authorized deity or force. And of course, the beating has to be connected with a legally-recognized, tax-exempt religion."

"The Founding Freemasons thought of just about everything. In-freaking-credible attention to detail! It makes me proud to be American, so help me God and hope to die."

"Leafy, do me a favour — *please* don't sing the national anthem again."

"Oh, say can you see . . . ."

Beefy knew that while Leafy's cacophonous rendition of Francis Scott Key's epic poem was super-hard on the ears, it was at least born out of true patriotism. He took his right hand from the steering wheel and, as he always did for the SSB, placed it with the utmost of solemnity over his heart.

* * *

Like all places of human incarceration, the first thing that hit you upon entering the Adelanto Detention Facility was the smell. The overall smell itself, of course, was indescribable by means of words; but it can be noted that the smell was a strange combination of many different smells, each one closely associated with the various residues from all the human bodily functions and the powerful chemical agents employed to clean them up. Leafy and Beefy had encountered the smell — or variations thereof — on many previous occasions, but they had never really gotten used to it.

The pair now stood in a small, darkened observation room that adjoined a larger, brightly lit interview room. They watched through the reinforced two-way mirror as Jesús Malverde was escorted into the interview room by three ICE guards, one at each arm and another slightly behind with a taser aimed and ready to fire. Although Malverde's official status was that of an 'undesirable alien' and he had not been charged at this time with any crimes within the United States, the guards were taking no chances with 'El Carnicero'.

He was dressed in a standard fluorescent orange jumpsuit, with white disposable slippers on his feet. Over his head had been placed a translucent spit-bag elasticised around his neck. Around his waist was fastened a sturdy leather restraint belt with affixed metal hoops, through which the chains of his handcuffs were cinched tightly to his sides. A short chain between his ankle manacles severely limited his movement and he was forced to move forward in an awkward, humiliating shuffle. The officers forced him down onto a chair and waited patiently for the homicide detectives to enter the room and begin the interview.

"Call this a hunch, Beefy, but I don't think we're gonna get too much out of this boy. The ICE guys have got him strapped up tighter than Hannibal Lecter."

"Well, we're here now. We've gotta do something. You got any ideas?"

"Short of waterboarding or nipple-twisting, I got nothing."

"Maybe he's not as bad as he looks," suggested Beefy, without much conviction.

"Are you freaking kidding me? He's *much, much* badder than he looks."

"Then I guess we'll just have to wing it. Come on marine-boy. *Semper Fidelis.*"

Beefy led the way as they walked through the interconnecting doorway into the interview room and the detectives sat down across the table from the prisoner. Beefy made the introductions and began the interview.

"Mr. Malverde, do you mind if we call you Jesús?"

A full five seconds elapsed before Malverde deigned to answer.

"You can call me what you want . . . just don't call me late for dinner."

Malverde's voice was soft, almost gentle, and it was a surprise to both detectives to hear it emanate from his huge, fearsomely muscled body. The spit-bag obscured the details of Malverde's face and it was impossible to read his expression. Leafy liked to watch people's faces, and he felt that the spit-bag actually put him and Beefy at a disadvantage.

"Jesús," opened Leafy. "Are you gonna be a civilized guy while we're here? We already know that you're a serious dude, a dude not to be fucked with. We also know that a guy like you is not going to do too much blabbing to the cops, unless of course it's to his advantage. So what I'm proposing is that even though me and my partner here have probably made this trip for nothing, we may as well all get comfortable while we're here. If you promise you'll be a nice guy, we'll get rid of the bag, loosen the chains a little, maybe get some sodas and smoke a butt or two. What do you say?"

Malverde thought about it for a moment and replied, "I aint gonna cause no trouble."

Beefy nodded to the guards and they removed the spit-bag and loosened Malverde's wrist chains so his hands could reach his face.

"What do you want to drink, Jesús?" asked Leafy. "And don't say a Long Island Iced Tea."

"I want a Coca-Cola. A *real* one, ice-cold. Not the shit they serve in the dining hall."

The most striking things about Malverde's face — and there were many striking things about his face — were his eyes. He had large, dark eyes with almost no whites showing around the edges. They were, in fact, quite frightening, and although something of a cliché, reptilian would be a most accurate word to describe them. Leafy now had second thoughts about unveiling the beast, but he could hardly reverse that decision at this point in the game.

Malverde's Coca-Cola arrived and Leafy lit up a cigarette and handed it to the chained man. One of the guards produced an aluminium foil ashtray and placed it down on the table. Even though the gang-banger was not being charged with any crime at this very moment, for the sake of due diligence, Beefy took the opportunity to remove his Miranda card and read Malverde his rights. Malverde sipped through his straw and once more savoured the great taste of America. He relaxed a little and leaned back in his chair.

"I like you guys," Malverde stated. "You come straight to the point. No fucking around, no bullshit. I respect that . . . because that's how I like to do business. So now that we're all sitting here nice and chilled out, what do you wanna talk about?"

"Jesús," said Beefy. "I'm gonna be right up front with you. Rosita has been arrested and charged with numerous firearms violations. Now, the problem I got with that is that I don't really think those weapons belong to her. I also don't think that she personally is much of a threat to society. So, if the person who really owns those guns were to come forward with the truth, well, that would get your little Rosita off the hook. Do you see where I'm going with all of this, Jesús?"

"Oh yeah, I see where you're going all right. Life with no chance of parole. Or maybe even death row."

"Like, we don't know how much Rosita really means to you, Jesús," said Leafy, lighting up a smoke of his own and ignoring Malverde's pessimistic, if not insightful, analysis. "But those poor kids . . . it's gonna be rough on them. What with Daddy being deported and Momma doing hard time, they'll probably be split up and just bounced from institution to institution. They *are* your kids, aren't they, Jesús? Your flesh and blood?"

"Oh yeah, they're my blood all right."

Leafy lit another cigarette with his own and handed it to Malverde.

"So what do you think, Jesús? Can you help Rosita and the kids out here?"

"She knew what she was getting into when she hooked up with me. She's a big girl."

"Maybe she is, but what about Carlos and Gabriela? Don't you think they're a little young to be punished for your sins?"

"What can I do?" asked Jesús with a shrug of his almighty shoulders. "It's out of my hands."

"What can you do?" asked Beefy. "Christ Almighty, Jesús, you could try stepping up to the plate!"

"Lord have mercy, Jesús," said Leafy. "You could try manning up!"

"Jesus, Mary and Joseph, Jesús," said Beefy. "You could try facing up to the truth!"

"Great God in Heaven, Jesús," said Leafy. "You could show some fatherly concern!"

Malverde laughed in the detectives' faces.

"You guys are funny. I know what you guys want from me. I mean, do you think I'm stupid? You wanna tie me to the chopper. There's no way, José."

The whole thrust of the interview so far was to get Malverde to admit ownership of the AK-47, and it was irksome to the detectives for an interrogation subject to be so perceptive about their stratagems. Up to this point, there had been no reference to the Hollywood Sign murder, but it was clear that Malverde understood that was the main reason for this interview. It was equally clear he would say nothing to incriminate himself with regard to that event, no matter what the consequences for his children and their mother.

Leafy and Beefy had hit brick walls like Malverde before and regrettably, such obstacles were oftentimes insurmountable. Despite his thuggish appearance, Malverde was a pretty smart and cunning character, and it was obvious he had earned his PhD in street smarts in a hands-on fashion. Despite these hurdles, Leafy was determined to walk away with something tangible from this encounter and he decided on a different angle of attack. He lit up yet another cigarette and handed it to the gangbanger.

"Do you want another Coke, Jesús?"

"Sure, amigo, I'll take whatever you got on offer."

Beefy sensed that his partner had some sort of inspiration and he leaned back in his chair content to just listen for a while.

"Jesús," began Leafy, holding the gangster's unnerving gaze. "Do you know what the word 'hypothetical' means?"

"Some of those big-assed gringo words aint exactly my sort of thing, if you know what I'm saying."

"Fair enough. Do you mind if I explain it to you?"

"Knock yourself out, Detective Green. Who knows? Maybe it's a word I should know about."

"It's *definitely* a word you should know about. If I told you a hypothetical story, that means that story is based on guesswork and there is no solid evidence to support the facts of the story. The story may or may not have really happened. Sometimes it's helpful not to be too specific about the details in a hypothetical story so a person who is listening to that story can make comments about the story without getting themselves into trouble. Are you with me so far, Jesús?"

"You're pretty good at explaining things," commended the gangbanger, "you should have been a teacher."

"Okay. Now I'm going to tell you a hypothetical story: Recently, a young woman was shot and killed. This woman was not a bad person, and there appears to be no one in her life who would want to hurt her. No motive could be found to explain why the shooter killed her. The investigators are guessing that she was shot accidentally. In other words, the perpetrator did not intend to kill this woman."

Leafy paused to gauge Malverde's reaction, and while the features of the killer's face were about as expressive as Darth Vader's in a high-stakes poker game, his cold, dark eyes sparkled with interest. Malverde was actually enjoying matching his wits with the detectives.

"But the thing is, Jesús, the shooter did intend to kill somebody. And not only that — and this is where this hypothetical story gets really interesting — the investigators are fairly certain the shooter was a paid assassin. Okay, so that's the end of the story, at least as far as the hypothetical investigators are aware. This is all purely hypothetical, of course, no names or places mentioned."

"That was a good story," Malverde responded, nodding in approval. "Maybe a little sad for a soft-hearted guy like me . . . but I always did like a good murder-mystery. The trouble is I still don't get what your hypothetical story has got to do with me."

"All right, Jesús, I'm going to spell it out real simple for you. We know you're not going to accept ownership of the chopper and we also know you're not going to 'fess up to no murder. Those two things are now history. They're off the table so let's just forget about them. So, moving on . . . I told you a hypothetical story and in that story there were two things that the hypothetical investigators needed to know: the hypothetical name of the intended victim and the hypothetical name of the money-man behind the hit. So this is the deal, Jesús. If you could hypothetically come up with those two hypothetical names, without incriminating yourself in the least — because, of course, the whole story is purely hypothetical — then me and my partner here could hypothetically help Rosita out. Maybe talk to the DA and explain the situation. And who knows? Maybe she could get off with time served and six months of probation. That way she'd be back in her house and still with the kids. This is all possible, Jesús. Hypothetically speaking, that is."

"Detective Green," interjected Jesús. "I really could use another cigarette."

Leafy lit up another cigarette and handed it over.

"I like the deal," said Jesús, slowly exhaling the smoke through his nostrils. "Hypothetically speaking, that is. But to nail this thing down today I need more than you just helping out my family."

"Like what?"

"Like two cases of Coca-Cola every week and two packs of Marlboro per day for the rest of my stay in this shithole."

"Wait a minute, Jesús," protested Leafy. "Who do you think we are? The faith, hope and charity cops? And have you done the math on that? That's about fifty or sixty bucks a week times however many weeks you're gonna be here. Who in hell's gonna pay for that? I know me and my partner can't afford that."

"It's all right, Holmes, I know you're just a pair of penniless cops. It just so happens I can afford it and my homies will bring it to me. You just make sure it's all stamped and approved by ICE."

"I don't see a problem with that," stated Leafy, extending his arm to shake Malverde's hand. "Have we got a deal?"

Malverde reached out and gripped Leafy's hand, giving two firm shakes and then releasing it.

"You might want to get your notebook ready," suggested Malverde. "Okay, the hypothetical name of the hypothetical intended victim is . . . Hugo Fürst."

"You go first?" queried Leafy.

"Hugo Fürst . . . with an umlaut."

"You go first with an omelette? What the hell kind of name is that? I thought we had a serious deal going here, Jesús."

"I am being serious. That's his hypothetical fucking name. I'll spell it out real simple for you: H-U-G-O F-U-R-S-T. Hugo Fürst. An umlaut is those two dots you sometimes see above a letter."

"Okay, now I get it."

"The name of the hypothetical guy who put out the hypothetical hit is hypothetically known on the streets as Binder Dundat."

Leafy was familiar with this particular name and did not have to query its spelling.

"There you go, Detective Green, I kept my side of the bargain. You make sure you keep your side. And just remember, we shook hands on the deal. Plus, I've still got the whole ESBSB posse out there on the streets watching out for my interests . . . hypothetically speaking, that is."

Ignoring the implicit hypothetical threat, Leafy closed his notebook and looked directly into Malverde's deathly eyes.

"It's okay, Jesús. We'll keep our side of the bargain. You take care now . . . coz you know how dangerous these kind of places can be."

"Don't worry about me, Detective Green," responded Malverde, flashing his demonic smile. "I'm gonna be just fine."

Leafy nodded to the guards and they replaced the spit-bag on Malverde's head, cinched up his wrist chains and shuffled him out of the room.

Immediately, Beefy stood up and pulled out a hermetically sealed evidence kit from his jacket pocket. Both detectives tore open the packages containing sterilized surgical gloves and then wriggled the gloves onto their hands. While Leafy held a specimen bag open, Beefy placed Malverde's drinking straws inside and sealed it shut. They did the same with Malverde's cigarette butts. The day before, they had tried to persuade a judge to issue a court order that would force Malverde to give up a DNA sample, but the judge had turned them down flat, citing an almost complete lack of evidence against the gangbanger. For all El Carnicero's cunning, the two cops had lulled him into a false sense of security and had sufficiently distracted him into making a serious legal blunder. The straws and cigarette butts had been discarded by the suspect and were now deemed to be public property. And while they were not an equally acceptable evidentiary alternative to a court-ordered DNA sample, they could be used as probable cause to get a warrant to obtain a more official specimen of Malverde's DNA.

* * *

The morning excursion to Adelanto had been productive, but pinning the N. Emma Johnson murder on Malverde was by no means a slam-dunk. His hypothetical statements — assuming that they were even truthful — could not be used against him, and at the very most implied only that he had some knowledge of the crime. Much more definitive, in an evidentiary sense, was Malverde's DNA sample, which had already been sent to the lab for profiling.

It was just past lunchtime and Leafy sat at his desktop computer checking an emailed report that had arrived in his inbox fifteen minutes after they had left for Adelanto. Having read and reread the report, he printed out a hard copy for his partner to peruse. Beefy, who had slipped out to do some personal errands, arrived back at their workstation and immediately noticed their ageing laser printer noisily going through its routine.

"What's shaking? Besides the printer, that is."

"C&N breaking news: The President was unexpectedly admitted to Walter Reed National Military Medical Center this morning. But thankfully it's not too serious. Apparently, they found a very small conscience growing right next to his heart, but it can be removed very easily by means of a simple, painless procedure at any one of the many Conscience Removal Clinics in and around the District of Columbia."

"All right," said Beefy. "I'll rephrase my previous question: What's shaking that might actually pertain to police business and in particular, the Enema Johnson case?"

"BATFE came up with two comparison hits on the AK shell casings."

As a matter of procedure, the forensics team had run comparison tests on the shell casings through the LAPD's local database, which had all come up negative. The casings had then been forwarded to the National Tracing Centre in Martinsburg, West Virginia — a Bureau of Alcohol, Tobacco, Firearms and Explosives facility — for a more comprehensive nationwide search. Leafy, who strongly disapproved of convenient, overly abbreviated acronyms, always referred to the ATF as BATFE.

Beefy picked up the single-page report from the printer bay and read through its contents. The first recorded incident related to the AK-47 had occurred three years ago at a cocaine stash house on the outskirts of El Paso, Texas. Two people had been killed and three others severely wounded in what the ATF classified as 'an internecine, cartel-related narcotics robbery'. The second incident had occurred some fifteen months ago, and while it was no less brutal than the first, it was significantly more mysterious. It had taken place on a desolate stretch of Highway 190 in the mountains west of Death Valley some ten miles east of the town of Panamint Springs, California. A rented Winnebago recreational vehicle travelling westbound on the highway had been attacked by at least two armed assailants, causing the camper to tumble over three hundred feet to the bottom of a boulder-strewn canyon. The vehicle had been occupied by a family of four, a mother and father and their two teenage daughters. The family had been nearing the end of a two-week vacation, having visited several well-known tourist attractions including the Grand Canyon and Death Valley. The three females had all been killed, either by gunfire or by the impact of the crash. Inexplicably, the emergency response team attending the scene had not recovered the father's body and he had never been heard from since.

"What do you think?" asked Leafy.

"It looks like the AK was a burner after all . . . but that's no reason to associate these crimes with our case. That gun might have gone through a dozen owners before it arrived in LA."

"That's very true," responded Leafy, no longer able to contain an irritating, triumphant smirk that threatened to envelope his face. "But I think you might be missing something here, old pal."

Beefy read the report again, but nothing new jumped out at him from the page.

"Look down at the bottom of the page at the list of the victim's names," prompted Leafy. "*You go first with an omelette.*"

"Hugo Fürst . . . my God, Leafy, they wiped out his whole family! This is un-*freaking*-believable."

"I know, but one way or another they didn't manage to nail Hugo. It turns out that El Carnicero was actually telling us the truth."

The two lapsed into silence as they struggled to make sense of this latest revelation.

"So what have we got here?" Beefy asked and then answered. "The same assault rifle was used fifteen months apart in two failed attempts to assassinate Hugo Fürst. In both cases, collateral damage was of no concern to the killer or killers. We strongly suspect that Malverde was the shooter in the second attempt and we have tentatively tied him to the murder weapon."

"Then it's a reasonable assumption to say that Malverde was also involved in the first attempt," stated Leafy, following Beefy's train of reasoning to its logical conclusion.

"Unless something comes up to change our minds," affirmed Beefy, "that's going to be our working theory. Man, we've got to nail this son of a bitch before he gets a free ride back to San Salvador."

"That's a big ten-four."

"So, extending our theory one step further . . . our new friend Hugo Fürst must be the running-man."

"Your reasoning is una-*freaking*-ssailable, big guy," said Leafy. "I'm thinking another internet search might be just what the doctor ordered."

Five minutes later and the two detectives had finished reading a condensed social media version of Hugo Fürst's biography. They had compared the picture of the running-man to several website images of Fürst and there was no doubt that they were one and the same person.

"This cat is one serious brainiac," observed Leafy with muted admiration. "He's got more letters after his name than a medium-sized can of alphabet soup."

Doctor Hugo Fürst, MD, BSc, PhD, Sterling Professor of Genetics and Professor Emeritus at Yale University, had been born in Vienna, Austria. At the age of fourteen he had immigrated with his parents and two siblings to the United States of America for a new life in the new world. His father had been a successful chemist and had been a strong influence on Hugo in his choice of making a career in the world of science. And now, in the present day, it was generally acknowledged by his contemporaries that Hugo Fürst was to the field of genetics as Stephen Hawking was to the field of theoretical physics. Not unlike Hawking, Fürst was a superstar of sorts, but only amongst the elite few who had chosen and understood his particular area of research.

"You know, Leafy, this is probably not Malverde's first job as a hitman. And, judging from his lavish lifestyle, I very much doubt that his services would come cheap. So why would anyone pay out some serious bucks to get rid of some geneticist that nobody except other geneticists has really even heard of before?"

Leafy had no substantive answer to the question and remained uncharacteristically silent. At that moment, three email messages simultaneously arrived in their PC's inbox.

"It never rains in da de da da," sung Leafy, forgetting the song's lyrics and tuneless as always, "and girl da de da da . . . ."

Leafy scratched the outer rim of his right ear with his left forefinger and left-clicked on the first message with his right.

"Forensics has a solid match on one of the sets of fingerprints lifted from BADASS 39: our good buddy, Jesús Malverde. They also found significant traces of gunshot residue in the trunk of the vehicle consistent with the chemical signature of the remaining rounds removed from the AK's magazine. No prints were found on the rifle itself."

"Yet another nail in Malverde's coffin," observed Beefy. "It's a step in the right direction."

Given the uncertain circumstances regarding their main suspect's residency in the US, the Department had agreed to pay out the extra cash required for a priority fast-track analysis of Malverde's DNA sample. Cutting through the scientific jargon, the second message informed the detectives that Malverde's DNA had indeed been found in the Dodge Charger, and, against all the odds, his DNA had also been matched to a sample of biological material located in a tiny crevice between the wooden butt stock and the metal frame of the AK-47.

"That's all we need!" cried Beefy, jubilantly. "Malverde's ass belongs to us!"

"High-five!" offered Leafy, lifting his right arm.

"No thanks. The old Mysophobia's taken a turn for the worse and I was forced to revise my policy on high-fives. Besides, it's kind of a silly, xennial thing to do."

"Fair enough. I just thought with all those exclamation points flying around you might be up for one," replied Leafy, slapping his partner on the back instead. "Things are finally coming together. I gotta tell ya, Beefy, I really thought that murdering basturd was going to worm his way out of all this. Too bad we're on duty, because this definitely calls for a shot of tequila or three."

"Basturd?"

"2X the asshole power of a basterd and 10X the asshole power of a standard bastard."

"That's a whole lot of asshole power. Aren't you going to check the last message?"

"Yeah, I guess I should."

The third email was from the Adelanto Detention Centre, and it read: 'We regret to inform you that detainee #1247, Jesús Malverde, was found dead in his cell at 11:47 AM today. A twisted bed sheet was found tied around his neck with the other end secured to the bars of the cell window. A full investigation is currently underway, but a preliminary post-mortem examination strongly suggests that Malverde committed suicide. We will keep you informed as to the results of the investigation.'

"What in the Donald's name is going on here?" shouted Beefy, displaying a level of astonishment and annoyance that was unusual given his normally laid-back personality. "Okay, now it's official: the Enema Johnson murder investigation is starting to seriously *piss me off!*"

Several other detectives in the room glanced in Beefy's direction, surprised and mildly concerned at his outburst.

"This freaking case," offered Leafy, as infuriated as his partner, but not quite enough to invoke any of the many aliases of the Lord of Darkness, "is up and down like a *whore's panties on payday.*"

CHAPTER FIVE

A Hollow-Eyed Crack-Head

Leafy Green and Beefy Goodness could not recall another homicide investigation that had caused them more frustration than the N. Emma Johnson case. Even their two unsolved cold cases had not been as bad, for the simple reason that no viable suspects had ever come to light. For all intents and purposes their current inquiry had been solved — at least in the sense of the trigger-man — and with such airtight and damning evidence against Malverde an arrest had been only a couple of hours away. And with the prospect of the death sentence on the table, it was not entirely beyond the bounds of possibility that the gangsta might have flipped on his co-conspirators. It was scant consolation that their killer was now dead, because although divine justice may have been meted out, the cause of earthly justice had by no means been served. And serving earthly justice was what Leafy and Beefy were all about.

That there was more to the case than met the eye was a gross misrepresentation of the situation, and by no means did they consider the investigation closed. The mere fact that Malverde had first of all been detained by ICE and subsequently drew his last breath one hour after they had interviewed him did more than raise a few eyebrows; it stunk to high heaven. The sinister undercurrents of the case were both perplexing and deeply troubling and served only to stiffen the detectives' resolve to track down Malverde's co-conspirators.

Even the suggestion that Jesús Malverde was in any way suicidal was a laughable idea, and the very concept was 'reductio ad absurdum,' as the Romans used to say. Malverde was still a young man; relatively healthy and wealthy; had no good reason to believe that a murder charge was about to befall him and he was as tough and cunning as a pack of rabid hyenas. In both a physical and psychological sense, the gangbanger was not only eminently well equipped to deal with whatever violent conflicts lay ahead of him, he was clearly the sort of person that would look forward to and indeed relish those conflicts as an integral part of his own savage existence. Therefore, Leafy and Beefy were absolutely certain that El Carnicero had not committed suicide.

Captain Calderon Casablancas — or Triple C, as Leafy and Beefy were prone to calling him, disrespectfully, behind his back — was the chief of detectives and a summons to his office, as opposed to a meeting with the lieutenant in charge of the Homicide Bureau, did not usually bode well for those that were summoned. As a general rule, Leafy and Beefy preferred to work on their own and were somewhat secretive — if not proprietary — about their oftentimes unconventional investigative methods. This was partly due to a broad streak of competitiveness that was intrinsic to both of the detectives' personalities and which greatly assisted them in maintaining their partnership at the number-one spot in the Homicide Bureau. The other reason for their tight-lipped approach was an inherent distrust of any police officer above the rank of lieutenant. This approach had garnered them few allies in the higher echelons of the LAPD, but their incredible batting average generally served to shelter them from negative fallout from above. But such was not the case on the afternoon of the third day of the N. Emma Johnson investigation as they stood in the captain's office facing down on Triple C.

"I see you guys have been doing that phony K9 routine again," observed the captain sourly. "You are aware that you're barely skirting the laws of entrapment, aren't you?"

"The legal department and the lieutenant gave us the green light to go ahead," replied Beefy. "The results should speak for themselves."

"Over a dozen handguns and an assault rifle were taken off the streets," retorted Leafy, not content with the results speaking for themselves. "Not to mention that the 'phony K9 routine' gave us the evidence we needed to well and truly nail our trigger-man."

Even for Captain Casablancas, it was difficult to find fault with results such as those. Instead, he decided to change tack, while at the same time stubbornly withholding any credit for the detectives' handling of the case thus far. For their part, Leafy and Beefy stubbornly withheld any verbal reference to Triple C's rank.

"I understand that your trigger-man is no longer in the land of the living," said Triple C. "So if you guys are so sure that he was your perp, I guess you will be moving on to the next homicide investigation. As usual, we've got murder cases piling up around our ears, and it sounds to me like you've cracked this Hollywood Sign thing wide open."

"We've still got a few loose ends to tie up," replied Beefy.

"Oh yeah," probed Casablancas, his expression and tone of voice highly sceptical. "Like what?"

"Like the fact that we have every reason to believe that other people were involved in the murder," stated Leafy, deliberately circumspect.

"Is this another one of your conspiracy theories, Green? Why can't you ever take things at face value? I mean, do you really believe that the Illuminati are trying to take over the world? Or maybe they're just trying to take over this investigation?"

In point of fact, Leafy did not believe in the Illuminati; but by the same token, neither did he disbelieve in it. In Leafy's world, just about anything was possible, but until such time as some tangible evidence was forthcoming, his belief remained in a state of suspension. While blind faith was not Leafy's main credo in life, he remained partially open to the power of suggestion. Triple C's question was a direct reference to a heated debate that Leafy had got into with another detective at a staff Christmas party some five years ago. Leafy had consumed a few too many margaritas and, just for the hell of it, had decided to play the Devil's advocate by arguing in favour of that particular conspiracy theory. Apparently, he had still not lived it down and he had long since resolved to never make that sort of mistake again around the office. Leafy's disdainful silence treated the captain's question with the contempt that he felt it so rightly deserved.

Beefy stepped in to smooth things over.

"Captain, we need more time. It's as simple as that."

"All right," conceded Triple C, after a few seconds of consideration. "I'm gonna cut you guys a little slack here. Go and tie up your loose ends . . . just make sure you don't hang yourself with all that extra rope."

Captain Calderon Casablancas turned his attention to some documents on his desk, the standard signal of dismissal for non-obsequious underlings. Leafy and Beefy made a hasty exit and took the elevator down to the homicide office. At their workstation, Leafy sat down in front of their PC and systematically erased the internet search history for the last three days.

"Leafy, you realize that the history remains on the hard-drive even after you hit the delete button, don't you?"

"Of course I do . . . but unless the Digital Forensics Unit gets involved, that should slow most people down who might want to pry into our business."

"Did ya forget to take your paranoia pills again?"

"It's just like antibiotics, Beefy, I've built up a resistance to them. You know what I think? I think we should go undercover for a while."

"You know, my dear Watson," replied Beefy, in an atrocious attempt to emulate an English accent. "I think that's a capital idea. It would appear that we can't trust some of our fellow constables."

Against department regulations — or for that matter, the law of the land — the two had set up an anonymous, untraceable internet and phone account in a false name, which they occasionally utilized to ensure the security of their most sensitive case information. They also used the account to make untraceable online searches and, of course, plain old phone calls. Except to bask in the sunshine of Leafy and Beefy's investigatory successes or, if the case just happened to involve some well-known member of the glitterati, it was highly unusual for Triple C to take an interest in the progress of an ongoing investigation. He was usually far too busy sucking up to his superiors or trying to figure out how to make the next step up the hierarchical totem pole to concern himself with the mundane minutia of the department's hoi-polloi. This was what had triggered both Leafy and Beefy's alarm bells, and, given the strange series of events that was the N. Emma Johnson case, their secretive approach had just become even more secretive.

"What do you think that self-serving prick wanted, anyway?" asked Leafy, sotto voce.

"I think he was on a fishing expedition."

"Okay. So did he hook a marlin or a minnow?"

"I'm pretty sure he got skunked, but it really doesn't matter. You heard what the man said. He's giving us some more rope. So let's get out of here and see how long it takes to hang ourselves."

"That, my dear Holmes," replied Leafy, in a flawless rendition of a lisping upper-class British accent. "Sounds to me like a perfectly *scwumptious pwoposal.*"

* * *

There had been no rain for several weeks, and the whole of southern California was now in a state of drought. With the reservoirs severely depleted and wildfires raging ever closer to urban areas, the governor was on the cusp of declaring a state of emergency. The intense heat of the day, coupled with the desiccating effect of the Santa Ana Winds, had left the inhabitants vulnerable to dehydration and heatstroke, with the government at both municipal and state levels issuing health advisories on an almost daily basis. It was now official: all was not well in paradise. Bottled water was being shipped in and distributed to the most affected areas, but at a rate far outpaced by the demand. Especially vulnerable were the very young and the very old; and of course, the countless homeless people who had little respite from the extreme moods of Mother Nature.

For nearly a hundred years, the name Skid Row has been synonymous with the poor and disaffected people of the nation, a place that signifies the lowest rung on the societal ladder, the very antithesis of the American Dream. The physical reality of Skid Row is different to what some people might imagine and consists of a fifty-four block area in downtown Los Angeles bordered by Third and Seventh streets to the north and south, and Alameda and Main to the east and west. Because many of the social services specifically designed to help the poor and disaffected are located downtown, it is only natural that people requiring such assistance would congregate in an area like Skid Row where these services have been available for many years. And no doubt, the powerful and all-pervading doctrine of the NIMBY will ensure that Skid Row will remain faithful to its reputation and location for at least another hundred years or so. In the twenty-first century, the social services have increasingly placed more emphasis on rehabilitation rather than just the provision of food and a place to sleep. Several non-profit organizations had adjusted their policies accordingly and now offered twenty-four-hour services as opposed to just a meal and a bed. One such charitable institution was the Last Chance Mission run by the fiery Evangelical Protestant minister the Reverend Abigail Brown.

The Reverend Brown was a small African-American woman in her early fifties with short, iron-grey hair. Dressed in a smart black trouser suit and with a large silver cross hanging from a chain around her neck, she emanated an aura of strength and intelligence. She also happened to be one of Leafy and Beefy's most highly valued confidential informants, and they had sought out her counsel on many occasions over the years. She was not a paid informant, at least not in the financial sense of the word, but she did require a QPQ for her services. That usually entailed Leafy and Beefy leaving a token charitable food donation and also listening to one of the Reverend Abigail Brown's brutally-honest, politically-charged ad lib sermons. The detectives had been sitting in the minister's small, stuffy office for the last fifteen minutes and with relief they sensed that her holy diatribe was mercifully winding down.

". . . and for every so-called 'winner' in America, there are at least ten thousand losers. Our social structure has regressed into a Darwinian doctrine of 'might is right', where only the most fearsome and loathsome creatures in society are allowed to survive and flourish. In that respect, the Eye of Providence — or if you prefer, the 'all-seeing eye of God', which of course, is a pagan symbol that has nothing to do with decent Christian principles — printed above the pyramid on the back of our almighty dollar bill has been conveniently blind since well before the Declaration of Independence. Anybody with even half a dozen functioning brain cells must realize that *greed* is the superglue that bonds our society together in this great land of the free. A quick visit to Skid Row — or indeed any of the numerous other ghettos, 'hoods and inner-city human trash-dumps that are scattered across our nation — should convince even the most sceptical of souls of the self-evident truths inherent in my words. To base the social dynamics of our entire culture on the single premise of enormous short-term profits for the fortunate few is not only an affront to the teachings of our Lord Jesus Christ . . . it is a wholly unsustainable political concept that will inevitably lead to the societal disintegration of this great country."

Leafy and Beefy knew better than to comment at this final stage in the ritual and contented themselves with a sage nod of their heads in appreciation of the minister's harsh wisdom. The righteous fury in the

Reverend Abigail Brown's eyes slowly subsided and she favoured the detectives with one of her rare and mirthless smiles.

"So, detectives. How can I be of assistance to the Los Angeles Police Department?"

Leafy proffered two pictures of Hugo Fürst to the minister, one from Fürst's internet profile and the other the webcam image captured at the Hollywood Sign.

"We're trying to find this man, Reverend. His name is Hugo Fürst."

"You go first?" queried the minister. "Well, I have to say, that's a very strange name."

"*Hugo Fürst*, Reverend, with an umlaut."

"You go first with an omelette? I'm sorry, detectives, but I'm not really following you."

The reverend favoured Leafy with an uncomprehending, slightly apologetic smile.

"No problem, Reverend, I'll spell it out for you: H-U-G-O F-U-R-S-T. Umlauts are those two dots that you see above vowels on Swedish restaurant menus."

"Okay. Now I get it. Well, he certainly has a distinctive face," commented the reverend, as she scrutinized the photographs. "But I've never seen him around here. Is he a criminal?"

"No, he's not, Reverend," replied Beefy. "He's actually a well-regarded research-scientist, but we're 99 percent certain he's a homeless person at this present moment."

"Poverty can be thrust upon us at any time, no matter how well-regarded or successful we think we are, Detective Goodness. We would all be wise to remember that."

"We also think his life is in imminent danger, Reverend," added Leafy. "So there is a certain amount of urgency to our request."

"I understand, detectives. Leave it with me and I will see what I can find out. May God bless and protect you both."

* * *

According to the late Jesús Malverde, the money-man behind the attempted assassinations of Dr. Hugo Fürst was Binder Dundat — the first syllable of his first name pronounced like the word 'sin' and the second syllable pronounced like the word 'care' — a man who might best be defined in the words Winston Churchill used to describe the country of Russia: a riddle wrapped in a mystery inside an enigma. In spite of Dundat's well-documented public persona, nobody — except perhaps the intelligence community — knew exactly who he was or from whence he came. Because of the lavish Bollywood-style television commercials promoting his franchise of hot and spicy Asian fast-food restaurants, in which he himself occasionally played a starring role, Binder Dundat was a recognizable minor celebrity on the west coast of America. Handsome and debonair, talented and witty, he had charmed the pants off several Hollywood starlets, or so the west-coast tabloids had dutifully reported.

After leaving a few slightly dented, discount-priced cans of beef ravioli at the Last Chance Mission's food bank, Leafy and Beefy had spent the rest of the afternoon diligently researching what little was known about Binder Dundat, utilizing their private internet account and surreptitiously calling in favours from trusted law-enforcement sources across the state. As in all unsolved homicides — and they still classified the N. Emma Johnson case as such — the investigation would progress in ever-widening circles around the nucleus of the victim. From previous experience, they knew that extreme discretion was now a necessity because the higher up the food chain they climbed, the more influential the feathers that might be ruffled.

It was 9:45 AM on the fourth day of the case and it was Leafy's turn behind the wheel. Heading west along Ventura Freeway the rush-hour traffic was still heavy, but the radio reported no major snarl-ups and vehicles moved at a good pace towards the Pacific coast. The detectives ere heading to the El Ricacho Country Club just outside the town of Calabasas where they had arranged to meet Dundat before he headed out for his daily foray onto the links.

The small profile they had compiled on Binder Dundat was divided into two categories: the indisputable facts and the unproven allegations. And perhaps somewhere in between, amidst the layers of hype, myth and downright fiction, the inner truth of the man might be found.

The facts were as follows: He had legally entered the United States three years ago on an Indian passport with the stated intention of exploring business opportunities between North America and the sub-continent. His provable net worth was such that the USCIS had practically laid out a red carpet and a ticker-tape parade upon his arrival. He had quickly set up shop in the Los Angeles area and from there had taken the first steps in the forging of his curry-flavoured empire. His three-pronged marketing strategy had been simple and effective. Firstly, he had overcome the American aversion to anything that tasted even remotely weird by simply Americanizing the exotic flavours. Secondly, he had appealed to the innate macho-competitive spirit of the American people by daring them to climb ever higher on his numbered scale of spicy-hot delicacies. And lastly, he had flown in several big-name female Bollywood stars for his TV commercial extravaganzas, thus presenting to the American public the innate sexuality of the Indian culture. It was a win-win-win situation, and his franchise had taken off in a big way. On a more personal note, Dundat was a confirmed bachelor playboy, an avid and talented polo player and was possessed of a toffee-nosed English accent that he claimed was the result of his education in the hallowed halls of Eton and Cambridge, although no records appeared to exist of his alleged sojourn at either of those institutions.

On a darker note came the long list of unsubstantiated, quietly whispered allegations, some of the highlights of which were as follows. It was suspected that he had simply purchased his Indian citizenship in some untraceable bureaucratic transaction and that his real national roots lay closer to Pakistan or even Afghanistan. It was suspected that he had close ties to international terrorism, including organizations such as Al Qaeda, ISIS and especially the Taliban. It was suspected that he was the American point man for an Afghani/Pakistani cartel that was responsible for the new wave of cheap high-quality heroin that was now flooding the streets of several American cities and that he had been involved in the deaths of countless people, including several American citizens. The rumours and speculation went on and on, but the bottom line was that the authorities appeared powerless with regard to Dundat's alleged transgressions. It was also abundantly clear that he was not the sort of guy that any sensible person might want to unduly annoy. This last point was by no means lost on the detectives, but they were obliged to follow the leads wherever the leads chose to take them. While dealing with dangerous criminals was standard operating procedure for Leafy and Beefy, the terrorist element infused an added measure of caution to this particular facet of the investigation.

With time in hand, Leafy was content to cruise along in the trucker's lane at a steady 55 mph, deliberately allowing his mind to drift from the serious business of interviewing Binder Dundat.

"The LA Times says there's a ton of evidence that the President is secretly an orange supremacist."

"Oh yeah, I've heard of them," replied Beefy, absently. "They occupy the very top tier on the bigotry scale, spend a lot of time lounging around on tanning beds and they want to bring back those old-school lightbulbs. Right?"

"Amongst other things. What do they call those lightbulbs? Incan . . . incandescent."

"Incan descent? I don't think so. I'm pretty sure they're more like Aztec descent. Or they could be Mayan descent. But they're definitely not of Incan lineage."

"Sure. Mayandescent lightbulbs. Why not? That's what Thomas Edison invented and that's what the orange supremacists are all about.

And talking of the President . . . I watched an interesting interview with a bunch of people who voted for him in the last election. The interviewer asked them: 'What if the President stood on Fifth Avenue and swung a new-born puppy around by its tail while taking a leak on an old, handicapped, homeless woman and screaming at the top of his lungs that Jesus Christ was nothing more than a dilettante, socialist asshole.' So this one lady answers from the group: 'Well, puppies at that age can be very wilful and sometimes they need some strong discipline. It's just like they say: spare the tail and spoil the puppy.' Then this guy from the group pipes up: 'Homeless people should make more of an effort to better themselves. And besides, most of them just pretend to be handicapped to get money from us decent folk. The President is just trying to help her understand how much of a loser she is and how truly worthless she has become to both herself and the American people.' Then the same lady cuts back in: 'I'm an evangelist and you've got to realize that on rare occasions, the Messiah did show a bit of an . . . *ugly side*, considering he was the son of God. Remember when he kicked all those merchants out of the temple? Not exactly a ringing endorsement for capitalism and the American dream.'"

Leafy lapsed into silence.

"So what's your point?" asked Beefy, on the cusp of irritation.

"No real point. Just shooting the breeze. Trying to lighten the load a little."

"So are we finished with the President-bashing?"

"Well . . . not quite. I see that yet another woman has come forward and accused him of sexual assault," he stated, continuing — just for the sheer hell of it — to pick away at the scab of this particular unhealed wound. "How many women is that now? At least thirty. Right?"

"Stick of gum?" replied Beefy, proffering his brightly coloured pack of Jewcy Fwuit in what he knew deep down was a futile effort to distract his left-leaning partner.

Leafy took a piece of the chewing gum, braced the steering wheel momentarily with his left knee, unwrapped the gum, put the gum in his mouth, crumpled and discarded the wrapper onto the back seat, replaced his hands on the steering wheel and began to chew. Beefy remained silent, soaking in the parched highlights of the scenery through the passenger-side window. But as always, Leafy wouldn't — or perhaps couldn't — let it go that easily and he rubbed a little salt into the same wound.

"Actually, this lady is a pretty famous writer and she accused him of out-and-out rape. It's not often you hear that about one of our sitting presidents. I mean, messing around behind the first lady's back, well that's just standard operating procedure, par for the course and no big deal. But not rape. That's a Class A felony, for heaven's sake! Oh, and by the way, whatever happened to your MAGA ball cap? I haven't seen you wearing it lately."

Beefy had actually caught the aforementioned ball cap in mid-air as the then presidential candidate had flung a bunch of the red hats into the audience at a primary campaign rally aboard the USS *Iowa*, a decommissioned battleship permanently moored at the Port of Los Angeles. The republican detective had told everybody who would listen about the fortuitous event on the WWII warship and had occasionally proudly worn the hat with its bold, meaningless slogan around the homicide office. But as the ever-worsening scandals had continued to plague the billionaire's presidency and the evidence had inexorably mounted about his racist tendencies, Beefy had stopped wearing the hat and generally began to favour sports over politics as a subject of polite conversation.

"It's total fake news," Beefy finally supplied, forced yet again — like so many others who had voted for the Grand Old Party in the last presidential election — to either turn a blind eye or attempt to defend the allegations. "The media's out to get him. Besides, the President said she's not even his type."

"So what does that mean? He only rapes women that *are* his type?"

"You're twisting his words. That's not what he meant."

"Okay. So what you're saying is that the media somehow persuaded some thirty women to lie about the President," said Leafy, pushing the saline seasoning envelope just a little bit further. "For some reason or other, Beefy, I find that kinda hard to swallow. I mean, that would take quite a bit of organizing, don't you think? A whole bunch of different media outlets bribing or even coercing all those ladies — who apparently don't even know each other — to diss the President like that."

"Like I said, it's all fake news. How do you know what's true? If you and me believed everything we heard, we'd never solve a single crime. The important thing is that the economy is peaking out right now. Lowest unemployment rate in years. Our pension funds are safe and secure. What's not to like about that?"

"C&N says the tariffs might trigger a recession."

"Pinko-liberal, far-left horse-poo-poo," huffed Beefy.

"How about the Access Hollywood video?"

"Nothing more than 'boy talk'. Total fake news."

"The Steele Dossier?"

"English fake news."

"Russian election interference?"

"It's possible, but it was more likely Ukrainian or Chinese interference."

"That's not what the US intelligence community says."

"Yeah well . . . the spymasters get things wrong now and again."

"Collusion with Putin?"

"Deep-state hoax."

"Affinity for tyrants like KJU and MBS?"

"With Kim in the nuclear club and a fifty-billion-dollar Arab arms deal at stake, what choice has he got but to love those guys and do a little international ass-licking?"

"The DPRK called the President a dotard."

"I still don't know what that means."

"Penile dimensions proportionate to hand size?"

"Who knows?" answered Beefy, giving serious consideration to the question. "That could well be true. It just so happens that I've got really big hands."

"Two-hundred-million-dollar inheritance?"

"Fake news. He's a self-made man. Everybody knows that. It's just an amazing coincidence that his father happened to be a filthy rich real-estate tycoon."

"Deutsche Bank money laundering?"

"Anybody up for another witch-hunt nothing-burger?" enquired Beefy, holding up two fingers on either side of his head in an eloquent air quote gesture.

"Multiple bankruptcies?"

"That's just a hyper-partisan baloney sandwich," Beefy responded, sticking to the food-themed defence, "courtesy of the Democrats and their buddies in the crooked fake media."

"Income-tax evasion and charity fraud?"

"All right, Leafy," proclaimed Beefy, with an air of finality and a dangerous glint in his eyes. "Now you're starting to get under my skin."

Leafy had taken it to the limit yet again, and having pushed all the wrong buttons, this was the mission-abort signal for which he had been waiting. He promptly changed the subject.

"Did you see that?" asked Leafy, drawing his partner's attention to a mid-sized RV that had momentarily drawn level with the Crown Victoria before slowly overtaking them on the inside lane.

"See what?" asked Beefy, glad to talk about anything else, no matter how inane or preposterous that subject may turn out to be.

"It's the *freaking* Hardassians!"

Well accustomed to his partner's weird obsession with the lives of local celebrities, Beefy paid little credence to the remark.

"Sure it is," he commented, in a voice heavily laden with irony. "The Hardassians always roll around the freeways of LA in a mid-nineties Winnebago with a rusty propane tank and Arizona plates on the back."

"I'm telling you, it was them. That old hippie-mobile is the perfect camouflage for those guys," Leafy declared, as he swung the big sedan out into the passing lane. "I mean, what better way to keep a low profile?"

"Oh yeah . . . that's what the Hardassians are best known for: keeping a low profile. It's not even 10:00 AM yet, Leafy. Everybody knows they don't get out of bed 'til way past noon."

"Sometimes they have to get up early if they've got a morning pedicure appointment . . . or a photo shoot in San Francisco."

Leafy gunned the big V8 in hot pursuit of the Winnebago and finally settled in some fifteen feet behind the ageing camper's corroded rear bumper.

"Leafy, what the heck are you doing?"

"What does it look like I'm doing? I'm keeping up with the Hardassians."

"Did I ever tell you that you're a complete dingle-berry?"

"Let me just check the data-bank . . . huckle-berry, chuckle-berry, google-berry, wiggle-berry, snaggle-berry . . . but no, I don't ever remember you calling me a dingle-berry, never mind a *complete* one. But you know what? It has a nice ring to it, kind of festive sounding in a cutesy-wutesy sort of way. I'll tell you what: I'll accept my new dingle-berry status if you take back that mean old snaggle-berry dig. You know, man, it's kind of hurtful making fun of a person's overbite like that."

"It's a deal."

"All right, cool. Now let's go and have a chat with this spicy-hot terrorist guy."

* * *

The El Ricacho Country Club was a pretty swanky affair. Vehicular exotica littered the sprawling parking area, each car meticulously aligned in its assigned space by smartly dressed, uber-deferential valets. Upon arrival at the gated main entrance, the detectives had flashed their badges to the armed security guards, but that had not been deemed sufficient to allow them access to the property. Only after a thorough scrutiny of both officers' IDs and two phone calls to confirm their appointment did the electric gates slide open, and under the watchful eyes of guards, dogs and cameras, Leafy waved off the valet service and drove clear across the car park and right up to the main clubhouse. He reversed the Crown Victoria into one of the premium parking slots reserved for the club's highest flyers and placed a blue plastic sign on the dashboard. It read: LAPD VEHICLE. DO <u>NOT</u> TICKET OR TOW.

Inside the main reception area, the detectives had once again been asked to produce identification and, after a five-minute wait, had been duly escorted to yet another, slightly smaller reception area. By now, both detectives were feeling frustrated by all the obstacles and bull-crap that seemed to be flying in their direction and Beefy was starting to get downright irritable.

"Who does this guy think he is? Prince Harry and Meghan Markle?"

That Beefy appeared unaware of the physical impossibility of his comparative proposition was a strong testament to the depth of his complete and utter discombobulation.

"And don't forget little Archie," Leafy added helpfully.

"What we should have done," said Beefy, ignoring Leafy's helpful contribution, "is have the uniforms pick him up with lights flashing and sirens blaring and drag his sorry ass downtown to our neck of the woods."

They both knew that at the present moment, Beefy's alternative scenario — although hugely attractive — was not a viable option; but the detectives felt a whole lot better with the mere voicing of the idea. There was no getting around the fact that, at least for his first interview, Binder Dundat would be on his own turf and squarely in the heart of his comfort zone. And the detectives would have to deal with whatever disadvantages that may entail.

"David Hasselhopper."

"What about him?" asked Beefy, unable to completely erase the impatience from his voice.

"Nothing. It's just that the mere mention of his name usually gets a big laugh. I thought it might lift up your spirits a little."

"Normally it would, but not this time."

"Okey dokey. Then can you guess who this is? 'Russia, if you're listening . . . .'"

Beefy's thunderous expression strongly indicated that Leafy's query had not come anywhere close to lifting Beefy's spirits.

"Okay then, how about this: Do you have to own a cow to be a cowboy?"

"Yes," replied Beefy, with absolute authority and without hesitation. "Either that or you have to have unrestricted access to one on a regular basis."

"How about if you just own a horse?"

"Then you'd be a horseboy."

"A Stetson?"

"A hatboy."

"A Colt 1873 Single Action Army?"

"A gunboy."

"Chaps?"

"No comment."

Leafy considered his partner's responses and realized that he was slightly surprised at how compelling this previously unconsidered bovine limitation to being a cowboy was in actuality. But something didn't quite jive with Beefy's take on the western genre and he plunged blindly on with his questions.

"So was John Wayne a cowboy?" he asked, trying to somehow trip Beefy up.

"You better believe it, Pilgrim."

"Like, I don't know this for sure . . . but I'm pretty certain Big John didn't own any cows. At least not in Hollywood."

"Maybe not, but he had unrestricted access to them."

"How could you possibly know that?"

"It only stands to reason, Leafy. Name one self-respecting ranch-owner in the USA that wouldn't have granted John Wayne complete and unrestricted access to one of his cows if John Wayne had knocked on his ranch-house door at any time of the day or night and asked for such access to be granted forthwith and without demur?"

"How about Clint Eastwood?"

"Definite, no-messing-around cowboy."

"Not a cow-owner per se," supplied Leafy, doing his best to follow the course of Beefy's reasoning, "but a default cowboy by virtue of the self-respecting ranch-owner clause . . . right?"

"You got it, muchacho."

At long last, one of the club's uniformed minions arrived and escorted them into what appeared to be a large banquet hall where Binder Dundat and a group of what Leafy and Beefy assumed were Dundat's 'people' were seated around a circular table beside a wall of windows that overlooked an incredibly green golf course. State-enforced restrictions on the use of water had been in place for several weeks, but they clearly did not apply to the El Ricacho Country Club.

"Welcome, gentlemen," greeted Dundat, as he rose from his chair and favoured them with one of his famous, devil-may-care, impossibly white-toothed smiles. "I apologize profusely for any delays you may have experienced, but as I am sure you are both aware, such inconveniences are all part and parcel of doing business in the twenty-first century. Can I offer you some refreshments? Or perhaps a little brunch?"

Leafy and Beefy sat down in two unoccupied chairs that had been placed diametrically opposite Dundat's position, after which their gracious host followed suit.

"I'll take a large iced-latte," said Leafy, breaking his two cup rule. "Double-cream, no milk and easy on the coffee. *Actually* . . . on second thoughts, make it triple-cream with extra sugar and lots of coffee. And oh yeah, maybe just a sprinkle of shaved dark chocolate on the side. And a cinnamon stick to stir it all up. Oh, and just to be on the safe side, you'd better bring a couple of napkins as well. *S'il vous plait*."

"I'll take a glass of water," said Beefy.

From long habit, both detectives made a mental note to pay for their beverages on the way out. As the waitress served them their drinks, they checked out the sheer luxury of their surroundings, from the enormous gastronomic breakfast buffet laid out on adjacent tables to Dundat's retinue of hangers-on, which included six beautiful young handmaidens — minus any sort of strange dystopian headwear — who were immodestly attired in the skimpiest of pool-side no-swim swimsuits. It was hard for two average Joes like Leafy and Beefy not to be seduced by the sheer self-indulgence of it all, but they were well aware of how the LA rich and famous liked to operate. This was all just a huge mirage custom designed to put the two penniless peon cops firmly in their place, while at the same time assessing their amenability to any subsequent acts of bribery. If nothing else, the well-heeled and deep-pocketed could be very predictable when it came to dealing with the common folk.

As had already been arranged, Leafy opened up the interview, determined right from the get-go to imprint the full authority of the LAPD upon the proceedings while at the same time reminding Binder Dundat that a visit from the 'Death Police' was not something to be taken lightly.

"Mr. Dundat, I'm Detective Jerome Green and this is Detective Sergeant William Goodness of the Los Angeles Police Department's Homicide Bureau . . . ."

Dundat's affectedly over-the-top British-accented voice cut right through Leafy's introductions. "Leafy . . . and Beefy, if I'm not mistaken." Dundat pointed at each detective in turn as he uttered their nicknames.

Although not a closely guarded secret, neither of the detectives' nicknames were exactly what might be called common knowledge. No references to the names Leafy and Beefy existed in either their military or police personnel files, and neither man had revealed them on social media. Only their old military buddies and a few close associates referred to Goodness and Green in such a manner. Given that this interview had been scheduled only the night before, to come up with such personalized information in so short a time indicated that Binder Dundat had considerable research resources at his disposal.

Leafy continued as if Dundat had not spoken. ". . . and we'd like to talk to you about a series of murders that have occurred over the last fifteen months."

"Fifteen months?" queried Dundat, with a puzzled frown. "I thought you were here about that unfortunate Hollywood Sign incident. If I'm not mistaken, that happened just a few days ago."

"Fifteen months is the timeline that we're currently working with," inserted Beefy, "but as we collect more evidence on the case it might turn out that the crimes stretch out over a much longer period of time. We're quite certain at this point in the investigation that the Hollywood Sign 'incident' as you call it is just one event in a series of interconnected events."

"I see," Dundat responded. "Then tell me this: am I considered to be a suspect?"

"At this stage," replied Beefy, deliberately formal, "we have no evidence to support a theory based upon your direct involvement in these homicides. Therefore, from an official standpoint, we do not regard you as a viable suspect."

"How about unofficially?" asked Dundat, favouring his retinue with a Donald-may-care smile that implied that he dealt with irksome officials on a daily basis and knew exactly how to handle them.

"In our world, Mr. Dundat," said Leafy, taking a sip on his latte, "everything is official. Your name has come up during the course of our enquiry and we are just following standard procedure. If you'd be good enough to answer a few simple questions, we'll be on our way and you can get on with the rest of your day. Do you mind if we do an audio recording of this interview?"

Dundat went into a whispered huddle with a man and woman that were seated on either side of him and then nodded in acquiescence to Leafy's request. Both the man and the woman were soberly dressed in business attire and they emanated the seriously careful demeanour of the legal profession.

"Fire away, detectives. I have nothing to hide, and you should be aware that I've always been a strong supporter of the noble cause of law enforcement."

"What is your relationship to Jesús Malverde?" asked Leafy, firing both barrels with his first shot.

Another quiet huddle with his lawyers ensued.

"I am reliably informed that Jesús Malverde happens to be the patron saint of the Latino gang culture. Apparently, he has been dead for many years and he went to his grave long before I ever set foot on American soil. So to answer your question, I have *no* relationship with that particular individual."

Beefy clarified his partner's question.

"We're talking about a different Jesús Malverde, a much more up-to-date version. Jesús Malverde 2.0, if you will. He claims you recently paid him to kill several people in multiple states across the US. Is there any truth to Malverde's statement, Mr. Dundat?"

Another quiet huddle with his lawyers ensued, this one slightly longer than the last.

"There is absolutely no truth to that statement," declared Dundat, maintaining his smile despite the shocking gravity of the allegation. "I have never met with, nor have I had any dealings with any person of that name."

Leafy pushed a little harder. "Have you any idea why Jesús Malverde would come up with your name — out of all of the names in this whole, wide world — as the financier of his killing spree?"

Apparently, Dundat felt confident enough to field this question without the aid of his legal counsellors.

"I am a high-profile TV celebrity, detectives. I would respectfully suggest that Mr. Malverde may well be guilty of pulling your leg . . . or in the American parlance, *yanking your chain.*"

"Funnily enough," said Leafy. "It did occur to us that Malverde might well be trying to misinform us — him being a criminal and all — and that's why we've went to considerable lengths to substantiate his claims."

From his inside jacket pocket, Leafy extracted a summary of the digital forensics report that Armand Hammer had prepared after conducting his analysis of the hard-drives of Malverde's computers and cell phones.

"Given your previous statements, Mr. Dundat," probed Leafy, as his eyes skimmed over the highlighted entries in the summary. "Can you explain why your personal email address and telephone numbers registered to yourself and to your company were found on Malverde's computer and phone logs?"

With this question, Dundat's legal confidence waned, and yet another quiet huddle with his lawyers ensued. This one, however, was longer than all the others put together. Several minutes stretched out before Dundat made his reply.

"All of my contact information is in the public domain. I get hundreds of emails and telephone calls each and every day, and the truth is, detectives, I simply can't keep up with my own soaring popularity. I assume that this Malverde fellow — not unlike my many other thousands of adoring fans — was merely attempting to congratulate me for being such a successful entrepreneur and to offer yet more praise for my spicy delicacies. I hope that clears up any confusion about my involvement in this tragic affair. And now, if you'll excuse me, I really do have do get out there and work on my putting stroke. There's a charity golf tournament coming up soon and I don't want to make a fool of myself in front of the police commissioner and the mayor. Gentlemen, it's been a most pleasurable and informative meeting."

With that, Binder Dundat rose to his feet, fastidiously wiped his hands on a napkin and led his people from the room.

"What do you think, Beefy? Was that enough rope to hang ourselves?"

"Not quite. But with all that name-dropping, I can feel the noose cinching a little tighter."

"Yeah, me too."

"I guess we should go pay for those beverages."

"I guess we should. Either that or we could just say *piss on it* for once."

* * *

Upon returning to headquarters, a total of eight voicemail messages awaited the detectives. Three were related to other cases and one was a reminder to Beefy from his wife of a family barbecue planned for that evening. The remaining four messages fell into that annoying category of providing no reason for the call, yet requiring a return call as soon as possible. In chronological order the callers were: Armand Hammer, the Reverend Abigail Brown, their divisional commander's secretary and Irma Manstein.

"My, my . . . we are popular today," commented Leafy. "It must be that new cologne you're wearing, Beefy."

"Well, it sure aint your boyish good looks. I wonder what the div-com wants."

"He's probably on the guest list for Binder Dundat's charity golfing soiree and just wants to make sure we didn't offend his host with any awkward, niggling questions."

"Maybe he's found out we've been taking beverage bribes," Beefy quipped. "I knew not paying for those drinks would come back to bite us in the butt."

There was no getting around a call from the divisional-commander's secretary, and Beefy called her back.

"You'd better get your game-face on," said Beefy. "He wants us upstairs like pronto, Tonto."

Once more, Leafy and Beefy took the elevator up to the rarefied floors of the top brass. Not unlike a doctor's office, no matter how well his schedule was running, there was usually a minimum ten-minute wait before underlings were allowed into the divisional-commander's presence. This time, however, the detectives were escorted directly into his office. Triple C and another man in a dark grey suit were already seated and the divisional-commander — bubbling over, as always, with his own patented brand of ersatz charm — gestured for Leafy and Beefy to take the weight off their feet.

"I know you guys are busy," said the div-com, with his well-practised, winning smile, "but there's somebody here I'd like you to meet."

Gesturing to the dark-suited man, the div-com completed the introduction.

"This is Special Agent Justin Case of the FBI. And these two officers are Detective Sergeant Bill Goodness and Detective Jerry Green, our MVPs in the Homicide Bureau."

The three nodded their heads in silent acknowledgement of each other's presence.

"I'll get right to the point," continued the div-com, switching to his well-practised serious face and directly addressing the detectives. "I have been reliably informed that the case that you guys are currently working — the Hollywood Sign killing — may have certain national and perhaps even international implications. As a matter of procedure, from this point on, the FBI will be assisting us in the investigation. I want you to apprise Special Agent Case of your progress to date and your plans for moving forward with the investigation. You *do* have plans for moving forward, don't you?"

"Oh yeah, we've got lots of plans," Beefy affirmed.

"And those plans are all about moving forward," added Leafy.

"Great stuff! Absolutely excellent work, detectives! Well, gentlemen, my schedule is an absolute bear today, so I'll let you go and get yourselves acquainted. And make sure you keep the captain here up to speed. Have a nice day."

Captain Casablancas remained seated while the FBI man and the two detectives left the room.

* * *

Special Agent Justin Case seemed like a real nice guy. This greatly exasperated Leafy and Beefy, because, as much as they resented his federal intrusion onto their home turf, they could find little wrong with him as a person. On the outside, Justin Case portrayed the stereotypical FBI image of the clean-cut, sober-suited agent but the detectives did not detect any of the arrogance and condescension that they had come to associate with the Feds. Justin Case was self-effacing, amiable and humorous, did not say lots of stupid things and was vastly apologetic for treading on the detectives' collective toes. He was also very generous with the federal government's money and had paid for a superb lunch for the detectives at a pretty decent Mexican restaurant in the downtown core.

Case was maybe an inch under six feet tall, a dark-haired, blue-eyed, even-featured Caucasian male with little that might make him stand out in a crowd. As likeably bland as he was, it almost seemed as if the head honchos had gone out of their way to select an agent who would specifically appeal to the two homicide detectives. With that firmly in mind, neither detective trusted him as far as they could collectively throw him, which was pretty far, but probably not far enough.

"So what are you guys suggesting?" asked Case. "That one of the Adelanto ICE guards took out Malverde?"

"We're not suggesting anything," replied Leafy. "But there's no way that boy did himself in."

"Okay, fair enough," the special agent relented. "I'll check into the USCIS investigation to see if anything's come to light. At the very least, the coroner's report should highlight any indications of foul play. So what did you guys get out of the Binder Dundat interview?"

Beefy fielded this question.

"Not too much. Been-There-Done-That is as smooth as a freshly ironed silk shirt. Between him and his in-house legal team, he's got a plausible answer for everything we threw at him. If there's any dirt to be dug up on him, we'll have to do it the hard way, with a pick and shovel and maybe some dynamite."

"I'll see if there's anything in his bureau file that might help you out. So . . . what's the next move for you guys?"

"We're gonna talk to one of our confidential informants," said Leafy, as he raised his lanky frame from the restaurant chair.

"And who might that be?" asked Justin Case with an affable smile.

"What exactly don't you understand about the word confidential?" replied Leafy with an equally affable smile.

"I'm just doing my job, detectives. I guess you guys had better get going. I mean, you wouldn't want to keep an ordained minister of the cloth waiting now, would you?"

"Thanks for lunch," said Beefy, ignoring the agent's foreknowledge of their plans. "And if you guys are picking up the meal tabs, maybe we'll catch you around suppertime."

"Well, it's like my mom always used to say," replied the FBI man. "The way to every policeman's stomach is through his oesophagus. You boys stay in touch now."

"That's an affirmative," affirmed Leafy.

Transitioning from the climate-controlled comfort of the eatery, the two detectives walked through the invisible, yet palpable, wall of heat onto the sun-seared sidewalk.

"Mother Nature is sure being a little bitchy lately," Beefy commented as they hastily made their way to the Crown Victoria.

"Bitchy? Momma Nature's being downright schizophrenic. In her present persona, she's a hollow-eyed crackhead turning tricks after midnight, trying to make a few lousy bucks for her next fix. And believe me, Beefy . . . Momma doesn't give one sweet damn about us kids waiting back at home."

CHAPTER SIX

#superscasty

Given the unusual amount of interest showering downwards from the top brass, coupled with the use of veiled keywords such as 'implications', 'complications' and 'considerations', Leafy and Beefy were surprised that they still held the reins on the N. Emma Johnson case. In the normal course of events, the powers-that-be would not have trusted two low-ranking, gumshoe cops with the handling of such an allegedly politically sensitive investigation. The only conclusion that the detectives could draw from the situation was that they were being set up, either for failure or to take the heat. While neither of those options were particularly attractive, they had no choice but to play along to the bitter end. That was the negative side of the equation. On the plus side, the sheer arrogance of the powers-that-be sometimes rendered them unable to discern the sharply honed perceptive abilities of the rank and file. And that was their big mistake.

They had called the Reverend Abigail Brown, but the business of saving souls was a time-consuming affair, and she had indicated that she would not be available until after the Last Chance Mission's supper rush-hour. So they had headed instead to the Gang Unit's headquarters.

"What's the word on the street, Irma?" asked Beefy.

Leafy, Beefy and Irma Manstein stood outside in the walled parking compound used to house the unit's vehicles. Irma's roughly hewn features reflected an uncharacteristic expression of concern, and she restrained her normally powerful voice to a conspiratorial whisper.

"I'll tell you what the word is on the street. This whole frigging building has been bugged. The telecom company came in yesterday and replaced all our computers and phones. They said the old ones were out of date, as if I didn't already know that. You know what it's like with the Department, Beefy, you've gotta fight tooth and claw to get a new box of paper clips around here, never mind a new phone. And now, right out of the blue, they upgrade all of our communications equipment."

"You're absolutely certain that the place has been wired?" asked Leafy.

Such was Manstein's concern that she forgot to insult Leafy in her reply. "Surveillance is what I *do*. Believe me, this whole place is wired for sound."

"Okay," said Beefy. "So who do you think is behind it?"

"Well it aint the freaking North Koreans, that's for sure. It's gotta be some branch of the government — *our* government, that is — and I think it has to be tied in to our mutual buddy: the late Jesús Malverde."

"So you heard about his suicide, then," observed Beefy.

"You bet I did. And that whole thing stinks worse than a platoon of hung-over marines after two days of latrine duty."

At that moment, the officers' collective attention was drawn to an unusual high-pitched motorized noise that cut through the everyday sounds of the city. Getting louder and louder, it seemed as if a large swarm of Nazi killer bees hopped up on crystal meth accompanied by a small army of drunken zombies wielding hand-held leaf-blowers were approaching the Gang Unit's compound from the south. A dark object suddenly appeared overhead, hovering some three hundred feet above the pavement level. It was a professional unmanned aerial vehicle of the sort used by filmmakers and photo-journalists to get overhead video footage. It consisted of eight tubular support struts emanating from a central hub like the spokes of a wheel. At the end of each one was a gasoline-powered motorized whirling rotor. Roughly four feet in diameter, it was painted black and it had some as yet unidentifiable pieces of equipment projecting down from its underside.

"I don't know what this clown thinks he's doing," commented Leafy. "They banned the use of drones within the city limits a couple of years ago."

The three officers watched in fascination as the screaming robot descended and took up station about thirty feet from them and maybe six feet above the top of the parking compound's concrete wall. Clamped between its two horizontal landing skids was a swivel-mount camera and what could now be clearly identified as an automatic carbine pointed directly at them.

"*Jesus Christ!* That's a goddamned machine gun. Take cover!" screamed Manstein.

But there was nowhere to take cover. It had all happened too fast and the three were caught out in the open. Behind the drone was a multi-storey wall of windows belonging to the office building across the street, and there was no way the officers could risk taking a shot at the sinister little aircraft. It hovered for another few seconds — plenty of time for its operator or operators to hit the firing command — and then rapidly ascended and was quickly lost from sight.

"That thing had us dead in its sights," said Manstein. "It could have taken us all out, no problemo."

It was not every day that they came eyeball to lens with a killer robot, and the three were visibly shaken. Beefy took out a notebook and jotted down a note for Manstein. It read: 'Me and Leafy are under surveillance as well. It's time to go old-school. The drone was some sort of warning. No more electronic communications. Meet us at the corner of Alameda and Third at 1900 hours. If you can make it just nod your head. Come on foot and make sure nobody follows you'.

Manstein read the message, nodded, took out a cigarette lighter and set fire to the note.

* * *

Leafy and Beefy had driven straight to the nearest muffler repair shop. Choosing not to officially identify themselves, they had feigned an exhaust problem and waited patiently in line with the other customers until their big Ford sedan had eventually been hoisted in the air. It had taken less than a minute for Leafy to locate the tiny tracking device that had been magnetically attached to the inner surface of the car's support frame. While Beefy had momentarily distracted the mechanics, it had been a simple matter for Leafy to reach up and remove the offending device and attach it to the underside of the car on the hoist beside them.

In of itself, finding and removing the tracking device had been a small tactical victory, a temporary respite from whoever it was that was trying to keep tabs on them. But the mere fact of its existence transformed unsubstantiated suspicions into cold, hard reality. As far as they were aware, neither Leafy nor Beefy had ever been the actual subjects of a surveillance operation before, and that knowledge only served to render their current predicament all the more disturbing. By the same token, it was also extremely aggravating.

With Leafy in the passenger seat, the detectives now waited on the street outside the Digital Forensics Unit's rear doorway for Armand Hammer to exit with his bicycle. Apart from the occasional overtime shift, the DFU operated during normal business hours and they expected Hammer to leave for home within the next few minutes. For the last hour they had tried to make sense of the situation, but with little success. More information was required before any factual determination could be made. They had compiled a list of people that they hoped could be trusted, and Irma Manstein and Armand Hammer were currently the only two names on it.

"It doesn't look like you'll be making that barbecue tonight, Beefy. Did you give the wife the heads-up yet?"

"No. She knows from long experience that there's only a fifty-fifty chance of me turning up for anything that involves our social life. Not only that, it's quite possible that Big Brother might be listening in on my land line."

"Man, let me tell you," growled Leafy. "It rocks my freaking socks to think we're being bugged. I mean, we're the good guys. Right?"

Beefy remained silent for the briefest of moments, but the slight hesitation to uphold his partner's proclamation lent weight to what he eventually said. "So you just take it for granted you're on the side of the angels? Like you've got a lifetime membership on the good guys' team."

"You bet your sweet ass I do," Leafy shot back, slightly taken aback by both the solemnity of Beefy's words and the darkness of his tone. "You wanna know why? Coz I *am* a good guy."

"But everybody thinks they're a good guy," countered Beefy. "Even the bad guys think they're good guys. I imagine that deep down even Dennis Rader and Gary Ridgway think they're good guys. Misunderstood, I'll grant you, but still good guys. How do you know you're not just kidding yourself?"

For a few long moments, Leafy had no substantive comeback, no snappy return; and his mind reeled as he attempted to understand and correlate the confusing events of the last couple of days. The more he thought about it, the more surreal the situation appeared. And now, even Beefy was starting to question the foundation of their reality. He came back to the 'Land of Leafy' the only way he knew how.

"Suddenly, the voice on the phone lapsed from a loud whisper to a deafening silence," murmured Leafy, in a well-executed, dramatically deep Scottish accent. "Here, Beefy, check this out: How many oxmorons does it take to make two plain-clothed city cops puke?"

"Oxymora."

"What?"

"The plural of oxymoron: oxymora."

"Get the hell outta here! That doesn't even sound like English," protested Leafy in a voice that said things were starting to return to some semblance of what he regarded as normality. "I'm calling you on that."

Beefy laughed for the first time that day. Back in Illinois, Beefy's mom had taught high-school English and over the years, had filled her son with several tons of grammatical minutiae.

"It's true."

"Okay, maybe it is true, but just for the record, I seriously doubt it. But tell me this: did you know that Neil Armstrong's famous moon-landing spiel was not the one he had been practising in the months running up to the Apollo Eleven mission?"

"No, I did not know that."

"Now, I might be paraphrasing a little here, but this is the gist of what he originally planned to say when his foot touched the lunar surface for the first time: 'One teensy-weensy, itty-bitty, roll em up and scratch your kitty step for man . . . one humongous, stupendous, enormous, ginormous leap for the USA.'"

"Okay. So why didn't he actually say that?"

"Who says he didn't?"

"*You* says he didn't."

"Oh yeah. You're right. I did say he didn't. Well apparently, for some reason or another, he had a bunch of stuff on his mind that day and he just forgot."

As Leafy reached for his phone to Google Beefy's unbelievable linguistic plurality claim, Armand Hammer came out of the building and spotted them right off the bat. He walked his bike over to their car.

"Bill! Jerry! I guess you guys got my message."

"We sure did, Armand," replied Beefy as the car window slid down. "So what's up?"

"Somebody's been trying to hack into the DFU's computer network. This isn't the first hacker we've had and it won't be the last, but it looks like this one was specifically targeting data relating to the Hollywood Sign homicide."

"But they didn't get into the system, right?"

"Through six of my best custom-designed firewalls? Not a chance," replied Hammer. "But I'll give them an A for effort. Anyway, it occurred to me that you guys might be able to help me track down these particular hackers, considering it was your case information they were trying to steal."

"Yeah, maybe we can," said Beefy. "But we can't talk about it right now. What are you doing later on, say around seven?"

"I usually take my dog for a walk after supper ... but if you've got some info on the hacker, just name the place and I'll be there."

"We'll see you at the corner of Alameda and Third. And don't use your bike, come on foot," instructed Beefy. "Just one more thing, Armand: didn't you say that flying drones is one of your hobbies?"

"You know me, Bill. If it's electronic and nerdy, I'm usually up for it."

Beefy handed Armand Hammer his phone, which had a picture from the gallery cued up on the screen that Beefy had taken earlier in the Gang Unit car park.

"You ever flew one of those puppies before?" asked Beefy.

"That's a heavy-lift, gas-motored octocopter ... *very nice*, but way out of my price range. And that's some pretty nasty hardware it's carrying. Where did you take this snapshot? At a military base or something?"

"I took that picture this afternoon, right here in downtown LA. Do you recognize the make or model? And from what you see there, is there any way we can trace the drone back to its owner?"

"Not really," replied Armand. "It looks like a pretty standard star configuration with no decals or logos. There are hundreds of websites offering custom and generic design plans. With a few basic mechanical tools and a bunch of spare cash, just about any fool can build their own drone."

"Oh well, it was worth a shot," said Beefy. "Make sure nobody follows you to the meeting and don't call us on the phone."

"Fair enough, I'll see you guys later," said Armand. He cinched up the chin-strap on his spacey-looking, streamlined bicycle helmet, mounted his bike and quickly disappeared into the rush-hour traffic.

* * *

Over the years, the Reverend Abigail Brown had developed her own network of informants amongst the street people of her flock. And while she herself had been unable to precisely pinpoint Doctor Hugo Fürst's location, she had eventually found somebody who could. The Reverend had introduced the skinny, dark-haired girl to the detectives as Trixie the Tagger. Trixie now sat in the rear seat of the Crown Victoria issuing terse directions to Leafy in the driver's seat.

"Slow down a bit," commanded the girl. "Okay, this is good right here."

Leafy stopped the car on a piece of wasteland beside the road. They were in an old industrial area on the East Side amidst the tangled ruins of several partially demolished factories. The place seemed to be completely deserted.

"We'll walk the rest of the way from here," directed Trixie. "And you'd better bring some flashlights."

It was just after 6:00 PM, with plenty of daylight left in the sky, but the detectives tacitly understood it would probably be wise not to question her instructions. Grabbing their flashlights, they alighted from the car and followed Trixie the Tagger into the tangled maze of debris. There was a strange, almost sinister atmosphere to the place. It resembled a film set for a futuristic, dystopian Armageddon flick, where even so close to the bustle of the city it seemed like a person could easily get lost forever.

Trixie halted in a cleared area in the middle of what was once a street. From beneath a piece of rubble, she produced a rusted iron bar that was maybe four feet long. With practised ease, she inserted the flattened end of the bar under the lip of a manhole cover and levered it to one side. Exposed was a circular concrete-lined shaft that led down into the bowels of the city's drainage system. Peering down into the dark cavity, it was now obvious to the detectives why they had brought the flashlights.

"Is this really necessary?" Beefy enquired of Trixie. "I don't *do* dark, confined spaces. There's gotta be another way we can meet this guy."

Standing a few paces away, Leafy was struck yet again by an overwhelming sense of unease about this case. And the peculiar scene that was playing out at that moment in front of his very eyes only added to that sensation. With the backdrop of a big red sun imperceptibly falling in the clear western skies, his heavyweight partner gazed down at the emaciated punk-Goth girl, his eyes beseeching her to come up with an alternate meeting place to this terrifyingly dark hole in the ground. With Beefy suffering from acute claustrophobia all his life, Trixie the Tagger had inadvertently stumbled upon his Achilles' heel.

"Maybe you should think about cutting down on the apple pie and ice cream, grandpa," suggested Trixie, with a look of disdain and a complete lack of empathy. "This is the only way that you're gonna meet The Doctor. Take it or leave it."

Leafy stepped forward and shone his flashlight down the shaft. Corroded steel rungs embedded into the concrete formed a ladder that reached down into the blackness. Both he and Beefy had concluded that the case would probably not move any further forward until they had spoken to the elusive professor.

"Hey look, man," suggested Leafy. "Why don't you hang tight here for a while? There's no point in both of us getting covered in crap."

Leafy climbed into the shaft before Beefy had a chance to reply.

"No guns," commanded Trixie.

"I bet ya Banksy doesn't talk to cops like that," commented Leafy, with his head and shoulders still sticking out of the hole. "You know, Trixie, bossiness is a very unattractive trait in a girl. Most boys don't really like it."

"No guns," repeated Trixie, wholly unimpressed with Leafy's sexist social advice.

"Go big or go home, right?" commented Leafy as he handed over his service weapon to Beefy and began climbing down the shaft, closely followed by Trixie the Tagger.

At the bottom of the shaft was a tubular horizontal tunnel, perhaps five feet in diameter, running in two directions, north and south. Before Trixie could proceed any further, Leafy placed a restraining hand on her shoulder.

"Hold up for a second, girl. There are a couple of things we gotta get straight here."

"Like what?"

"Like just a minute ago you called Hugo Fürst 'The Doctor'. What was that all about?"

"He is a doctor. So what?"

"Yeah, I know he's a doctor. But the way you said it kind of made me think that he's special to you, like he's some sort of 'important dude'. Do you know what I'm saying?"

"He is an important dude. That's why we all call him The Doctor. It's no big deal. He's gonna fix what ails us and open our eyes to the truth. *#superscasty.*"

"Hashtag superscasty? O-kay . . . so what the heck does that mean?"

"Are you ever out of touch. Don't you ever look around? The warnings are painted all over the city."

"Okay, Trixie. I admit: I'm older than thirty and kinda slow, so you'll just have to spell it out for me."

"It's superscary and supernasty combined. #superscasty, get it? You're a cop and cops ask lots of questions, but you still don't know what's really happening out there on the streets. If we don't get going right now, The Doctor will just take off and you'll probably never get another chance to talk to him."

Trixie took the southbound tunnel, which after three years of drought was as dry as the proverbial bone. For ten minutes or so, she led the way through a labyrinth of tunnels, confidently navigating her way through various intersections until they reached a nexus point where several smaller tunnels merged into one cavernous chamber. A meshwork of vertical and horizontal iron bars, partially clogged with garbage, prevented Leafy and Trixie from proceeding into the chamber. A faint glimmer of daylight filtered into the chamber from somewhere up above, and through the bars Leafy could barely make out several figures standing around in the filth and gloom.

"Doctor Fürst!" Leafy called out. "I'm Detective Green of the LAPD. I want to talk to you about what happened the other day on the side of Mount Lee."

Leafy's entreaty failed to elicit a response.

"I know your wife and daughter were murdered. I also know those murders are linked to the Hollywood Sign murder and that there have also been two attempts on your own life."

"There has been a total of four attempts on my life, detective, but who's counting?" replied Hugo Fürst as he stepped forward from the group. "And I sincerely hope you are not a part of the fifth."

"I made sure he's not packing heat, Doctor," supplied Trixie the Tagger, in a respectful voice that contrasted mightily with the contemptuous tone she adopted for the policemen. "He left his gun with his partner who was too much of a chicken-shit to come down here."

"Just for the record, Trixie, my partner's *not* a chicken-shit," corrected Leafy. "He just happens to suffer from claustrophobia, just like I happen to suffer from vertigo. So he does all the high-level work and I do all the low-level work and one way or another, we both get to Scotland at pretty much the same time."

"That sounds like a perfect arrangement, detective," said Fürst, his voice still liberally tinged with an Austrian accent despite his years in America. "Trixie, did you check him for any abnormalities?"

"No, Doctor, but I'll do it right now," said Trixie, as she rubbed her hand up and down in the crease of Leafy's rear end. "He's good to go, Doctor, clean as a whistle."

"Man oh man," declared Leafy. "This day just keeps getting weirder and weirder by the minute."

"Just a basic precaution, Detective Green," explained Hugo Fürst, cryptically. "Three years ago I stopped trusting in the system. As a police officer, you are very much a part of that system. Can you tell me why I should put any trust in you?"

Unused to answering such a profoundly weighty enquiry, Leafy had to think about it for a moment, but with his recent conversation with Beefy still fresh in his mind, he managed to summon up a vaguely cogent response.

"Because I'm one of the good guys . . . at least, that's what my mom always tells everybody."

"And I would be the last to dispute the accuracy of the maternal instinct," said Fürst, with a humourless chuckle. At that point and for whatever reason, the professor seemed to relax a little and lowered his guard ever so slightly. "All right, detective. What do you want to know?"

"Well, for starters, Doctor Fürst, who exactly is trying to kill you? And why are they going to all that trouble?"

"Several governments, including the US government, are out for my blood. They want to stop me from revealing to the world the paradigm-shifting results of my life's work."

"I know that your field of study is genetics, Doctor. But with all due respect, it's hard to imagine that analysing DNA could be that much of a threat to our national security. Unless, of course, you can prove that the last president was not an American citizen or that J. Edgar Hoover was really a communist."

"With sufficient data I could prove or disprove either of those theories. But in the light of my astounding discovery, both of those ideas pale into absolute insignificance. Do you know anything about genes, Detective Green?"

"As a matter of fact, I do. I know that a fifty-year-old pair of Levi's — in fair condition with the knees worn out and the leather patch still intact and attached — can fetch thousands of dollars on e-Bay."

"Scoff all you like, but believe me, there is nothing particularly amusing about my discovery."

"I'm sorry, Doctor Fürst, I meant no disrespect," explained the detective, realizing that he had better tone down his witty repartee if he wanted to obtain any useful leads from The Doctor. "It's been a bit of a hectic day for me and my partner and I was just trying to lighten the load a little. First thing this morning, our egos got trampled on by a Bollywood fast-food terrorist; then we found out that we are under surveillance by persons as yet unknown, but whom we think is our own government; then we got buzzed by a killer drone and now I'm standing here all scrunched up in a sewer having a conversation with a renowned scientist who may or may not have turned into a cult leader. But by all means . . . carry on with what you were saying."

"All right, I will do just that." Fürst paused momentarily, pondering how he could dumb down his explanation enough for this facetious dullard of a policeman to comprehend. "Can you name one other species on this planet that displays such a wide variation in both temperament and behaviour as the human species?"

Leafy lowered the pitch of his voice by half an octave before answering in a theatrically deadpan voice.

"All I know is that the people are represented by two separate yet equally important groups. Those who wear their ball cap visors in the forward position like an outfielder and those who wear their ball caps backwards like a catcher. These are their stories."

"Law and Order? Right?" digressed Hugo Fürst, despite himself and falling momentarily under Leafy's spell of supreme superficiality. "That used to be one of my favourite TV shows. Still is, actually . . . *Mein Gott!* I was just getting into my stride and you have forced me to veer away from the main thrust of my topic. Did your mother ever tell you that while you may well be a 'good guy', Detective Green, you are also an exceptionally irritating and frivolous man?"

"Well, funny you should mention that . . . ."

"That was a purely rhetorical question," rebuked Fürst in a sharp, professorial tone. "In other words, an answer is not required. Now please, I implore you: *be quiet and listen.* As one of the foremost authorities on the subject, I can assure you that there is no other earthly species that can compare with humanity's wide-ranging patterns of behaviour. And while it is most certainly the case that many other lifeforms exhibit complex social interactions, even the most intelligent of animals such as the higher primates, whales, dolphins, elephants and the like do not even come close to matching the extreme variability of human nature. Believe me when I tell you, Detective Green, there are no Adolf Hitlers or Mother Theresas in the rest of the animal kingdom. This cosmic gulf between absolute evil and absolute altruism in human nature has been the principal focus of my genetic research. On the surface, this extreme variability suggests that *Homines sapientes* are somehow unique amongst the terrestrial species and that that is the reason why they have come to dominate this planet's resources. This is a very tempting proposition to adopt — especially if you happen to be a member of the dominant species — but my exhaustive examination of this subject suggests otherwise. An analogy exists in the field of astronomy: up until the mid-nineties, it was still fashionable to think that our planet was a unique cosmic entity, but huge leaps forward in technology now tell us that there are thousands, perhaps even millions, of Earth-like planets scattered across our galaxy, let alone the known universe. Factor in the multi-universe theories that the physicists are currently bandying around and that figure turns into billions. So it is now a proven fact that planets such as our own are as common as muck and as numerous as grains of sand on a beach. The inescapable conclusion for any man of reason is that the universe abhors uniqueness of any sort, including exclusivity of life-forms. To put it all in a nutshell, it is my contention that humankind is not a single 'unique' species, but consists of two or more distinctly hybridized sub-species. This explains why we have on the one hand the Josef Mengeles and Jack the Rippers, and on the other, the Mahatma Ghandis and Dalai Lamas. Are you following me so far, Detective Green?"

"I was more of an artsy guy than a sciency guy at high school," replied Leafy. "But I think I got the general picture. Out of all the animals in the world, only people have real saints and sinners. And that's because the human race is not just one species, it's made up of two or more sub-species. What I don't understand, Doctor Fürst, is why the government really gives a damn about this and wants to shut you up. If what you say is true, then surely other geneticists around the world will eventually arrive at the same conclusions that you did and the cat will be out of the bag, so to speak."

"Other geneticists *have* arrived at the same conclusions," countered Fürst with exasperation, "and those who have spoken out are either on the run like myself or they have paid the ultimate price. A little research on your part will confirm the truth of what I am telling you. Bear in mind that there are only a handful of people around the world that are not only qualified, but have access to the required specialized data to arrive at such a momentous genetic determination. And when I say the government, I am referring to a handful of highly placed officials and their minions who control certain key agencies and who have long since sold their souls to the Donald. I don't know precisely who these individuals are because I was not given the time nor the opportunity to find that out."

For one long minute Leafy stayed silent and stared at Hugo Fürst through the bars. The doctor was not some nut-job or self-imagined 'expert' — he was the real McCoy. But what he was suggesting sounded crazy, the conspiracy theory to end all conspiracy theories. Compared to this, the alleged JFK assassination cover-up and the faked moon-landing hypothesis both looked like silly kindergarten romps. Even for Leafy, Hugo Fürst's conspiracy theory was a little too far out in left field, as it had not even had the chance to be bunked, never mind debunked and rebunked. He was now glad that Beefy — who had a zero-tolerance attitude to what he referred to as 'the paranoid delusions of the whacked-out left' — had not accompanied him to this meeting and he did not relish the prospect of relaying to his partner this particular aspect of the geneticist's message. Right now, Leafy needed some solid information that would move the case forward, while at the same time satisfying his down-to-earth partner's appetite for cold, hard facts.

"Doctor Fürst . . . I wouldn't think of disputing a single word you've said. That's because I'm just a cop and it's my job to catch those people responsible for not only your attempted murder, but the murder of your family, and the murder of an innocent young lady named Enema Johnson from Iowa. Can you come up with anything that might help me do that?"

After a few moments of silent consideration, Fürst reluctantly came up with something.

"I can give you a name. This person is aware of the situation as I have described it but approaches the problem from a completely different perspective to my own."

The geneticist produced a notebook and pencil, jotted down the name, tore off the page and passed it through the bars to the detective.

* * *

As a general rule, eureka moments were few and far between in the oftentimes laborious business of homicide; but as they waited near the junction of Alameda and Third, a graffiti-covered wall beside them proved the exception to the rule. The lower half of a mural depicting two surfers riding an enormous blue wave had been largely obliterated with gang insignia and street symbolism, most of it comprehensible only to the taggers and their cohorts. Amidst the scrawl, a simple, well-executed image had been painted and its crisply defined edges indicated that a template had been used in its creation. It portrayed a strange creature with a human head and what looked to be a reptile's body. Printed neatly beneath it was the caption: 'Is this your neighbour? #superscasty!' The detectives had noticed similar imagery in various locations across the downtown area, but until now, had paid them little heed. It was Beefy who noticed that this particular piece of graffiti had been signed by its creator with the initials TTT.

"It looks like our sweet little sewer guide takes pride in her work, Leafy."

"Yeah, I guess she does."

Leafy stared at the picture of the reptilian anthropoid and a feeling of anxiety rippled through his body. Instantly, he knew that it was connected to Hugo Fürst's research and that there was more to the doctor's current predicament than had yet been divulged.

"What's up with you?" enquired Beefy, attuned to his partner's moods. "If you're hungry, go and have a smoke. That usually curbs your appetite for a while."

"Something just clicked into place, Beefy. It's what Trixie told me down in the underworld. They've been warning us all along . . . but we just didn't see it."

"We didn't see what?"

"The writing on the wall."

"This is Mission Control to Space Cadet Green: you are cleared for re-entry. Have a safe and happy splash-down."

"I'm serious, man. But we'll talk later. It looks like we have company."

A dark, four-door SUV pulled up beside their vehicle and its front passenger-side window slid down. In the driver's seat sat Special Agent Justin Case with a serious federal expression on his face.

"What's shaking with you boys?" he asked.

"Not too much," answered Beefy. "What's shaking with you?"

"I changed the location of the meeting place. Right now, Manstein and Hammer are waiting for us at a secure location. I tried to get a hold of you but neither of your phones seemed to be in service. You should get them checked out with the phone company."

"Yeah, we'll get right on that," said Leafy, with restrained sarcasm. "This was supposed to be a private meeting. How did you find out about it?"

"You guys should get with the program," Justin Case stated, unable to restrain the condescending smile that threatened to envelop his entire face. "There's not too much that's private in this world anymore, gentlemen. Besides, did you *really* think that I'd rely on just a single tracking device on your vehicle? You were supposed to find the easy one . . . but you'll have to tear that old Crown Vic apart to find the other two, which incidentally are also fitted with microphones. Oh, and by the way, there are no spare vehicles in the carpool, just in case you were thinking of trading in your wheels."

"It looks like you've got all the bases covered, Justin Case," allowed Leafy. "Then I guess you'd better lead the way."

With Leafy behind the wheel, the detectives followed the FBI man's car as it headed out of the downtown area on East Fourth Street and eventually onto the eastbound lanes of the Pomona Freeway.

"What do you think so far?" asked Beefy, clearly unimpressed with the enforced change of venue.

"Well, my head says one thing and my heart says another."

"Oh yeah? Well, what does your gut say?"

"That we should have grabbed a pizza while we still had the chance."

"I'm not joking, Leafy. Maybe we should turn around right now and head back to headquarters . . . and to hell with Triple C and the div-com, we'll take this thing straight to the commissioner."

"And tell him what? That we don't trust the government anymore? That we don't like being messed around by the big, bad FBI? That one of his Pakistani celebrity golfing buddies is really a terrorist drug importer hiring Latino drug lords to kill renowned Austrian geneticists? *Come on*, man, keep it real. Even if we could track the commissioner down at this time of day, shortly after he's finished laughing his socks and his jockey shorts off, he'd ask us what exactly it was we've both been smoking lately and then politely suggest that our parents might have put a few parts-per-million too much disinfectant decolourizer into our collective gene pools."

Leafy could see that Beefy was getting angrier and angrier by the minute. It was a rare phenomenon to see him get really mad, and he worried that his heavyweight partner might either take a stroke or take a swing at Justin Case's smugly smiling face. Unused to being the calm voice of reason, Leafy tried to think of something to say that might deter him from either course of action.

"Beefy, we've got no real choice here. Let's just see how this all plays out before we do anything too drastic."

Some twenty minutes after leaving Skid Row, Leafy turned off the freeway onto a service road and followed the special agent's car into a large public parking lot. The Whittier Narrows Recreation Area consisted of fifteen hundred acres of parkland, lakes, rivers and trails, and was a welcome oasis of green within the urban sprawl of Los Angeles County. The park's sunset curfew was loosely enforced and kids still played in the fields and joggers and cyclists plodded along the meandering trails beneath the evening sun. It was a pleasant place, a stark contrast to the vandalized streets of Skid Row, but the pastoral illusion was slightly marred by a series of overhead power transmission lines that ran east and west through the park. The ground had been grassed over between the power lines' supporting towers, and picnic tables had been placed here and there for the park patrons' convenience. Gesturing for the detectives to follow, Justin Case headed towards one of those tables, where Irma Manstein and Armand Hammer awaited their arrival. After perfunctory greetings were exchanged and everybody was seated, Beefy turned on the FBI man.

"Just who the hell do you think you are? And who gave you the right to spy on us and change our arrangements? I ought to kick your ass all around this goddamned field."

"I don't blame you for being mad, Detective Goodness," replied Justin Case from across the table. "But before you resort to violence, hear me out first."

"And by the way, what's so damned secure about this location?" asked Beefy, not to be mollified so easily.

"It's a wide-open area randomly chosen by myself earlier this afternoon," explained the agent. "Therefore, I know that there are no surveillance devices installed nearby. But perhaps more importantly, we are directly beneath these high-voltage power lines."

"And that's supposed to mean something to me?" asked Beefy in a scathing tone.

"Bill, the wires give off a strong electro-magnetic field," explained Armand Hammer. "That blocks out anybody who might be trying to listen in with long-range surveillance equipment. Another added bonus is that it's tricky to fly drones with all these wires overhead. It's actually a pretty good idea . . . if you want a bit of privacy."

"Thanks, Armand," said Beefy. "Okay, Special Agent Case, let's hear what you've got to say."

"All right then. First off: I'm more than just a special agent . . . ."

"Let me guess," interrupted Leafy. "You're a *very* special agent."

"Nope."

"Okay then, you're an *extra* special agent."

"Not even close."

"How about . . . an *ultra* special agent?"

"Wrong again."

"I got! I got it! You're a *totally* special agent."

"You're way off base."

"*Extremely* special?"

"Completely incorrect."

"*Most* special?"

"Not even in the ballpark. Have you run out of dumbass superlatives, Detective Green?"

"Is that what you call them? Then yeah, I guess I have. So exactly how special of a special agent are you, Special Agent Case?"

"I'm a *supervisory* special agent. And believe me, that's about as special as it gets in the world of special agents. In fact, it's so special that the Bureau had to bring in a special company which specializes in coming up with special designations such as 'Supervisory Special Agent'. Am I making myself clear, Detective Green?"

"Not especially . . . but please carry on, Supervisory Special Agent Justin Case. And if you don't mind me saying so, can we quit beating around the bush and just cut to the chase?"

"Hey! Marine boy," advised Manstein. "Shut the *fuck* up and let the man speak."

"He's the one who's boasting about how special he is, Irma," replied Leafy, having the last word while at the same time heeding Manstein's grim advice.

"All right then," said the FBI man. "You want me to cut to the chase? Then this is the chase: all that stuff you've heard about on TV and in the news media about UFO sightings, extraterrestrials, alien abductions, Roswell, Area 51, the whole enchilada . . . well, guess what? It's true. At least, about 65 percent of it's true, discounting hoaxes, nut-jobs and mistaken sightings. It is a provable reality that alien hybrids are walking amongst us right now as I speak."

Beefy let out a derisive groan and shook his head in despair.

"*This* is what you brought us out here to tell us? A steaming pile of delusional sci-fi bull-crap? It feels like we're on some unseen episode of The X-Files. Leafy, let's get the hell out of here. We can still make the end of that barbecue . . . and you never know, there might be a few pork ribs left over. Beefy Goodness gets to eat a little porky badness maybe three times a year and I'll be damned if I'm gonna miss out on that because of this."

"I know where you're coming from, Beefy," soothed Leafy. "But maybe we should hang here for a little while longer. We'll grab some trans-fat and LDL cholesterol on the way home. My treat, okay."

Armand Hammer spoke up, intrigued by the FBI man's hypothesis.

THE SECRET SIGN OF THE LIZARD PEOPLE

"You said provable reality, Agent Case. What kind of evidence do you got?"

"Not the kind admissible in a court of law. Unfortunately, the bulk of my physical evidence has mysteriously disappeared, and what's left on file is anecdotal and largely uncorroborated. However, I got something here that you people might find persuasive."

Justin Case removed two eight-by-ten images from a plain brown envelope he had been carrying and handed them to Irma Manstein, who was seated beside him.

"This is a photograph from Jesús Malverde's autopsy," explained the FBI man. "And this is an x-ray of the same area of his body."

Without comment, Manstein checked out the images and passed them around the table.

"FYI: Malverde died of manual asphyxiation and his death has been officially ruled a suicide," continued Justin Case. "No evidence of foul play was found on his body or in his cell."

"FYI: excuse us if we don't buy in to the official version," stated Leafy. "And what exactly is this thing sticking out above Malverde's ass?"

"The coroner reported it as an 'anatomical anomaly,'" replied Justin Case. "To my eyes it's pretty obvious what it is: it's a tail . . . and more specifically, a *reptile's* tail."

The appendage in question projected as an extension of Malverde's coccyx, approximately six inches long and covered not with a normal human epidermis, but with shiny grey scales similar to the skin of a snake.

"So *that's* why graffiti-girl was touching up my rear end down in the sewers," said Leafy, with dawning comprehension, as he handed the images back to Justin Case. "And just to get this all straight in my head: alien reptiles are trying to take over the world, they are cross-breeding with people and the only way for us real humans to tell them apart is to grab a feel of their ass. That could make for some fairly embarrassing moments."

"Absolutely," agreed Justin Case. "But by the same token, not all of the alien hybrids have a physical deformity like Malverde's, so a tail can't be considered to be their only definitive identifying feature. Also, there are so many reptoids around right now that they often have trouble in definitively recognizing their own kind."

"Just for the sake of argument," said Manstein. "Suppose what you're saying is true. Why are you letting us in on the secret? And why isn't the FBI hunting down these . . . reptoids?"

"The reason I'm talking to you guys," explained Justin Case. "Is that the Hollywood Sign case has brought us all together, and to be quite frank, I don't know how far the rot has spread within the Bureau. From the information I have gathered, this is mission-critical time and the alien takeover is nearly complete. The truth is, I can't stop them on my own and I don't even know if they can be stopped. But somebody's got to try . . . and I guess I'm asking you guys to help me do it."

"So I guess you're responsible for bugging the Gang Unit's HQ," accused Manstein. "Not to mention the killer drone thing and trying to hack into Armand's computers."

"I had nothing to do with any of that," denied Justin Case. "All I did was put some tracking devices on Goodness and Green's car. And the only reason I did that was because I knew they had no intention of sharing their information with the Feds."

The group fell silent, with each of the police officers trying to absorb the FBI man's incredible revelations while at the same time assessing his true intentions. It was obvious to them all that unless Justin Case was some sort of cross between James Bond and Superman, he could not have been personally responsible for all of the events summarised in Manstein's accusation. If he was involved, it would have to be as part of a team; but his avowed mistrust of the agency he worked for and his claims of currently working covertly as an independent operator held a distinct ring of truth. It was Beefy who at last broke the silence.

"All right . . . it's Friday night and we've all had a long day. We've heard what you had to say, Supervisory Special Agent Case. So what exactly do you want us to do?"

"Give me two days of your time, that's all I ask. By all indications, the reptoids are planning something very big this weekend somewhere in the state of California. As of this moment, I don't precisely know where or when it's going to occur, but I'm fairly certain it's some sort of get-together, like a general conference or something. I need you guys to narrow down the details and help me carry out some kind of incursion. So what do you say, yay or nay?"

Armand Hammer was the first to respond. "If I'm hearing you right, after this weekend I'll know one way or the other whether aliens really exist. That jogger runs right up my alleyway, sports fans. I don't see how I can refuse. So my response is an emphatic *yay.*"

"Well, I'll have to make some drastic adjustments to my social calendar," stated Leafy. "But I guess I can fit it in."

Beefy and Irma stared at each other across the picnic table, looking for some facial clue as to the other's decision. Beefy was the first to cave.

"Okay, but I wanna make this absolutely clear: I'm only going along with this craziness because these events seem to be connected to the Enema Johnson case. So where do you stand, Irma?"

"If you're in, Beefy, then I guess I'm in too," replied Manstein. "Now, can we all get outta here?"

"There's just one last thing," said Justin Case, with a grimace of distaste. "We've got to make sure nobody here is growing a tail."

And as the sun finally dipped down below the western horizon, a casual observer glancing in their direction might well have observed the strange spectacle of five people taking turns to feel between the cheeks of each other's butts.

CHAPTER SEVEN

The Secret Sign

It was 10:30 on Saturday morning and Leafy and Beefy were headed north on Highway 101 towards the coastal town of Carpinteria, following up on the name Hugo Fürst had given up the day before. Riding shotgun in the Crown Victoria, Leafy perused the website that a brief internet search had produced on this particular individual.

"Ermine Stoat," he recited from his phone, picking out the keywords. "Crypto-zoologist, numerologist, mythologist, astrologist, ufologist . . . if it involves sketchy science and ends in 'ologist', it seems like this guy's got it covered. It says here that he runs an organization called the Database for Inexplicable Aerial Phenomena and Extraterrestrial Research . . . otherwise known as DIAPER."

"DIAPER?"

"That's what it says. Here, listen to this: 'DIAPER's primary function is to investigate an extra-terrestrial invasion utilizing reverse-engineered allen technology.'"

"Allen technology? That's gotta be a typo."

"Maybe so. But it looks like a pretty reputable website to me. It says here that the allens — who have become something of a hot-butter issue of late — are receiving their orders from an other-worldly sauce to achieve their objectives over at Oreo 51. Apparently, some of the allens arrived through inter-dimensional potholes which closed up shortly after their arrival and they are now left yawning for their home planet."

"Good grief."

"Check this out: Two fish and game wardens observed several uniden-tified frying objects hovering above a roadside concession stand near Roswell, New Mexico. Both wardens vociferously claimed that this event had been a clothed encounter of the turd kind. You know what, Beefy? If fish and game say they saw allen crafts frying over Roswell in a clothed encounter of the turd kind, that's plenty good enough for me."

"Did Hugo Fürst say how this Stoat guy might help us out?"

With their car still rigged with surveillance devices, the detectives had considered renting a car for a few days; but in the end they had said to hell with it, as it would be just more money out of their own pockets, and a different vehicle would by no means guarantee them their privacy. Instead, they chose to embrace the surveillance demon, and they assumed that every word spoken in the Crown Victoria was being monitored by Justin Case. They would play along with the FBI man's plan, but by no means did they fully trust him.

"All Hugo Fürst said," replied Leafy, "was that Stoat looked at the situation from a different perspective than what he did. It looks like we might be dealing here with a brainiac of a slightly different sort, Beefy. Maybe we should have brought along a little help from the Feds, you know, *just in case*."

"You mean like: *just in case* we can't understand all the big words?" said Beefy in a voice clear and loud for the sake of the microphones. "Or *just in case* we need somebody to pay for lunch?"

"All of the above."

The intense heat had by no means diminished, and the mercury presently hovered in the low nineties with the promise, yet again, of triple-digits on the Fahrenheit scale by the early afternoon. With a few more miles left of their journey and the air-conditioner running full-tilt, Leafy pulled out yesterday's edition of the *Los Angeles Daily News* from the back seat of the car and turned to the entertainment section. No matter how busy they were, it had become a weekly ritual for Leafy to narrate his own commentary of the highlights of the celebrity news as if he was reading it from the newspaper.

"It looks like they had an NRA charity bachelor auction for ageing newscasters at the Hollywood Bowl. Wilf Blitzkrieg was unable to attend, of course, but Shawn Vanity, Smucker Carlsen and Phil O'Really all strutted their stuff up and down the catwalk to the tumultuous applause of the well-heeled and high-heeled ladies of LA in this admirable and worthwhile cause. The talent and evening gown sections were absolutely adorable, it says, but it was the final bikini round that clinched it for the overall winner. Smucker raked in a cool one hundred and twenty-two bucks and was so overwhelmed with his victory that he wet his bikini bottom and had to be carried off the stage by Sean and Phil. All money raised will go to the NRA Executive Retirement Fund."

"Now that's what I call a worthwhile cause. And good old Pox News. They sure do know how to pick some good-looking dudes for their anchormen."

"Roger that. Here's another interesting article: three northern gold prospectors — thought to be lost forever — were recently rescued from the depths of Sierra Praline's vagina during a routine check-up with her gynaecologist. Praline's PR people released a statement saying that she is overjoyed that the prospectors survived their nightmarish ordeal and hopes that there are no hard feelings and that they will still vote for her in the next gubernatorial election. She added that they are welcome to keep any items of misplaced jewellery that they may have found in that dark and terrible place."

"All things considered, that's mighty white of her," allowed Beefy. "Maybe she can get the GOP to throw a tea party in their honour."

"That would be the patriotic thing to do," affirmed Leafy. "Maybe they can even get the Ukrainian three amigos to attend?"

"Once again, I have to point out that you are not just some under-the-weather young canine, Detective Green, but that you are in fact one very, very sick puppy," stated Beefy, smiling despite himself. "Is that it for the celebrity news?"

"Not quite. Charlie Spleen and Creeper Sunderland have agreed to take Justen Bleeper under their wing and show him how to act like a real bad boy. Apparently, throwing eggs and saying the N-word just doesn't cut it if you want to be an accredited member of BLOBBA."

"Okay, I'll bite," relented Beefy, after a short pause. "What's BLOBBA?"

"The Big League of Bad Boy Actors. I thought everybody knew that."

"Somehow that one must have slipped right under my RADAR, clear over my SONAR and totally through my LIDAR. So where exactly does this Stoat guy reside?"

"Up in the hills above the town," stated Leafy, as he consulted his newly updated turn-by-turn GPS navigation app on his phone. "Just keep driving and I'll tell you where to go. It's all right, man, I've got it covered."

"Sure you do."

After getting lost several times in the maze of dirt roads that snaked through the arroyos and canyons of the Coastal Range, they eventually stumbled upon the entrance to the old Stoat homestead at some fifteen hundred feet above sea level. Taking in the cactus and the rock and the desert scrub, it was hard to imagine how the original settlers had managed to eke out a living in that harsh and barren terrain. Driving past the shiny metal flying-saucer mailbox, Beefy steered the Crown Victoria slowly and carefully along the potholed driveway until they finally reached Stoat's residence. The place had a distinctly hippy-like, flower-child feel to it, with a couple of shabby greenhouses leaning against the side of the old stone ranch house, some solar panels on the roof, a small windmill generator spinning in the breeze and several psychedelic banners and signs strewn around the property proclaiming peace to mankind and a general and heartfelt affection for marijuana. In stark contrast to the haphazard and slightly run-down atmosphere of the property, a late-model Range Rover sat parked beside the house, sheltered from the elements beneath what looked to be a newly constructed carport.

Leafy and Beefy alighted from their car and took a moment to take in the magnificent ocean view. A voice sounded from behind them.

"On a really clear day you can see all of the Channel Islands, even San Miguel."

The detectives turned towards the voice and observed a tall man in his early thirties with a moustache and beard and long dark hair done up tightly in a ponytail. He was simply dressed in an untucked Superman tee-shirt, beige cargo shorts and open-toed sandals and bore a striking resemblance to any one of a dozen actors who had played the starring role in movies about the life of Jesus Christ. Both detectives were struck by some indefinable essence that emanated from the man. Perhaps it was the set of his features or the innocence of his smile, but an overwhelming and almost palpable sense of peace seemed to hang in the air that surrounded the ufologist. There was clearly something special about Ermine Stoat.

"Ermine Stoat?" enquired Leafy, as a mere formality, because he had instantly recognized the man from his online picture.

"That would be me," replied Stoat, with an open-handed gesture. "Welcome to my humble abode."

"I'm Detective Green and this is my partner, Detective Goodness. Sorry we're late. The traffic was brutal . . . and it looks like somebody removed all the road signs from around here."

"Yeah, I guess I should have mentioned that when you called. We don't get too many visitors up around these parts, and us locals all know where we're going. Come on in out of the heat."

The interior of the house was pleasantly cool and the three sat down around an old, well-worn dining table. Ermine Stoat politely offered them refreshments, which the police officers politely refused.

"We don't want to take up too much of your time, Mister Stoat," explained Beefy. "We've just got a few questions and we'll be on our way."

"No problem," replied Stoat affably. "Fire away. And please . . . call me Ermine."

"Like I said on the phone, Ermine," said Leafy. "Hugo Fürst gave us your name. When was the last time you spoke with Doctor Fürst?"

"Last night, about an hour before you called. He was just giving me the heads-up that you guys might try to get a hold of me. As usual, the professor was right on the money."

"What's your relationship with Hugo Fürst?" asked Beefy.

"That's a very good question. To be honest, it would be easier to tell you what our relationship *isn't*. We're not really friends or colleagues or family or even kindred spirits. Strange circumstances have brought us together, and the shared knowledge of a terrible truth is our only bond."

"That sounds pretty melodramatic, Ermine . . . almost poetic," observed Beefy. "How did you two ever come to meet each other?"

"We met online, through the DIAPER blog. His world of academia not only refused to acknowledge his awesome discovery, they tried to suppress it. Consequently, he turned to my world."

"Then I guess you know that Doctor Fürst's family was killed and that he's now in hiding and in fear for his own life?"

"I'm well aware of his predicament," stated Stoat with a fleeting look of sadness.

"Then if you don't mind me asking," asked Leafy, "if you both share this so-called 'knowledge of a terrible truth', how come he's laying low with the sewer-people and you seem to be carrying on without a care in the world?"

"Because Hugo Fürst is mainstream establishment, Detective Green, whereas the people in the DIAPER organization are regarded as the lunatic fringe. He is a world-class geneticist with unassailable DNA evidence that the human race has been infiltrated by an alien species . . . and all we've got is a bunch of fuzzy pictures and eye-witness testimonies that even the most inept of lawyers would tear to pieces in any court of law in this land. There are lots of people out there like me, and if we were suddenly to be hunted down and killed, it would only lend more credibility to our claims. It's far better to let us 'crazies' rant on about our little grey men. On the other hand, there are very few Hugo Fürst's out there and that's why the reptoids want him dead. It's as simple as that."

Stoat's candid rendition of what he clearly regarded as the truth seemed both honest and more or less feasible to the detectives, and the three lapsed into a brief, thoughtful hush. With Hugo Fürst and Justin Case and now Ermine Stoat all essentially saying the same things, even Beefy's huge reservoir of scepticism seemed to have sprung just the tiniest of leaks.

"You really do believe that we're being taken over by aliens," said Beefy, with more than a smidgen of astonishment. "I mean, with all due respect, Ermine, you seem like a smart guy and you don't come across as crazy — at least, not out-and-out California crazy . . . ."

"Did you say California crazy?" queried Stoat, who appeared vaguely offended by the term. "You know, detective, you can't go around alliteratively applying the name of American states as qualifying terms for negative adjectives and then expect people to take your word as the gospel truth."

"Sure you can," put in Leafy, unable to resist a defensive riposte. "Alabama awful, Washington weird, Utah ugly, Texas terrible . . . Louisiana lousy, Nevada naughty, Massachusetts mad, Illinois irate, Oregon ornery and Arizona angry, to name but a few. That's how us cops see the world, Ermine. There's no rhyme nor reason to it."

"Well," replied Ermine. "We're going to have to agree to be disagreeable on that point."

"I couldn't agree more," concurred Leafy. "Now what was it you were saying, Detective Goodness?"

"I was just saying that I'm the sort of guy that needs some rock-solid evidence — something I can see or touch — before I can really buy into something as far out there as this alien thing."

"The only way to get solid evidence," replied Ermine Stoat, "is to capture a SNOTWAD."

"A snot what?" queried Beefy.

"A SNOTWAD. Something Not of This World and/or Dimension," clarified Stoat.

"You people at DIAPER definitely do not believe in tailoring your terminology to create slick, cool-sounding acronyms," observed Leafy. "I respect that. I really do."

"Thank you," responded Stoat with a beatific smile. "We try to tell it like it is."

Leafy smiled his appreciation and continued along Ermine Stoat's train of thought. "So does one of these genetically modified human reptoids that you mentioned count as a SNOTWAD?"

"No. A hybrid doesn't cut it. By its very definition, a SNOTWAD has to be a full-blown, no messing around extraterrestrial or extra-dimensional creature or thing. This particular species of aliens visits us only on rare occasions to monitor the progress of their grand project and they presently do not reside on our planet. DIAPER refers to them — just like the twelve million other American citizens who believe in them — as the Lizard People."

"Yeah. I've heard of them before," commented Leafy. "That English dude David Hiker, or whatever his name is, makes a pretty good living peddling that reptile stuff."

"We at DIAPER want the threat of the Lizard People to be taken seriously, so we don't really associate ourselves with his particular interpretation of the theory. Besides, the origins of the Lizard People go back thousands of years to the ancient civilizations of India, China and Greece. Kekrops — the founder of Athens — was half-human, half-reptile. There are various references to reptoids in the great sagas of the Hindu religion. Not to mention Eve mating with the serpent in the Garden of Eden in the Book of Genesis. The list goes on and on, but the bottom line is that the Lizard People have been coming here for a very long time. The planet Earth is too cold for them right now. That's why they've instituted over the past couple of centuries the process of global warming, so as to warm up the mean global temperature by five degrees Celsius. It is indeed ironic that the very same carbon that was scrubbed from the atmosphere and buried during the global warm-up of the Cretaceous Period — when reptiles truly ruled the planet — is now being dug up, burned and returned to the atmosphere so as to make the planet habitable for the reptiles so they can return once more to rule the roost. It doesn't sound like much, but five degrees is enough to kill off over half of the human race — and there are presently too many humans for the Lizard People's needs — while at the same time turn our planet into a reptilian paradise."

"When you say there are 'too many humans for the Lizard People's needs,'" asked Beefy, intrigued despite himself, "what exactly do you mean by that, Ermine?"

"With the exception of those who make a huge and short-term profit from the raping of our planet — many of whom are in fact reptoids themselves — anybody with even a crumb of intelligence can no longer deny that the human population is spiralling out of control and that the Earth's resources are being consumed and/or destroyed at an unprecedented and wholly unsustainable rate, much to the detriment of not only humans, but of most other living creatures on the planet. Global warming is happening right here in our own backyard. Even as we speak, California is burning, and marine life in that ocean out there has been reduced by 50 percent since the 1970s. Fifty percent, detectives! We now get hundred-year-storms every two or three years and the three of us are literally sitting here right now between the Donald and the deep blue sea. It truly staggers the imagination! The Lizard People presently regard themselves as the stewards of this planet, and just as we humans do to various animal species — supposedly in the 'best interests' of that species — the Lizard People are going to *cull* the human race. Additionally, a smaller human population will be much easier to control and far less prone to disease and major violent conflicts."

"But I still don't get why the Lizard People are here," probed Beefy, temporarily suspending his own doubts in the light of Ermine Stoat's sound reasoning and obvious sincerity. "What possible use are we to them? What are they after, Ermine, diamonds or gold or oil or something?"

Ermine Stoat lapsed into a brief silence and regarded the two LA cops with an expression of profound sorrow.

"Human beings," explained Stoat, "just happen to be the Lizard People's favourite food. In a galaxy where food planets are few and far between, the planet Earth is destined to become one of the Lizard People's cosmic burger joints. Hybridized humans — the reptoids — will not be on the menu, however, because they will be responsible for controlling the general population, not unlike the role that the Jewish capos played in the Nazi concentration camps . . . but on a much, much larger scale."

"If you ask me, Ermine, this whole thing sounds just a bit too complicated," held forth Leafy, half believer and half *advocatus diaboli*. "Assuming that the Lizard People are more technically advanced than we are, why don't they just mount a good old-fashioned invasion of the planet and get it over with, like the aliens have done in countless sci-fi movies?"

"They've already tried that. It was called the Second World War, where the fascist leaders were in actuality human-reptile hybrids. Of course, the Manhattan Project put a stop to all of that . . . and now that we humans possess nuclear weapons, it's far too risky for the Lizard People to try anything but a covert, bloodless takeover. The reason it has to be kept secret is to prevent mass hysteria breaking out amidst the human livestock populations and also to stop any one of several powerful nuclear nations interfering with either the global warming process or the hybridization program before they are complete and irreversible."

"Hashtag superscasty," mumbled Leafy.

"You better believe it," affirmed Stoat.

"Ermine," continued Leafy. "What if I told you that we have it on very good authority that something big is gonna be happening with the reptoids this weekend? It's some kind of alien general conference — a reptilian reunion, if you will — which, from what you're telling us, might actually involve a visit from the Lizard People themselves, and we're pretty sure it's gonna happen somewhere right here in the state of California. Can you tell us how we might pinpoint its exact location?"

"Sure I can," stated Stoat with absolute confidence. "This is America. Just follow the money trail."

"Can you be just a *little* bit more specific, Ermine?" prompted Beefy.

"The Westerly family. Is that specific enough for you?"

The Westerly dynasty was the epitome of old money on steroids, but with a distinctly Californian twist, possessing wealth beyond the wildest dreams of most of the regular, run-of-the-mill super-rich people. They had arrived from the East during the gold rush, with already deep pockets, and after quadrupling their fortune with the heavy, yellow metal, had soon moved on to the oilfields and eventually into real estate. The Westerly family was now the fourth largest private landowner in the United States — the largest in California — and were possessed of a diverse worldwide portfolio of lucrative business interests, with a special emphasis on the high-tech giants that inhabited Silicon Valley. The Westerly family kept a very low public profile and were extremely private — some said even secretive — about their business and personal dealings. As such, they were notorious for their litigious zeal when it came to defending themselves against anybody who would dare to impugn their reputation or attempt to tarnish their supreme social standing. Anywhere in the world, but especially in California, the Westerly Corporation was a force to be reckoned with. Easton

Westerly III was the family's ageing patriarch, a self-proclaimed philan-thropist and defender of social justice, who was now reportedly in failing health and confined to a wheelchair. It was rumoured that his daughter, Eleanor — referred to by most people simply as Nor Westerly — had recently taken over the reins of power.

"You know, Ermine," said Leafy, in a voice brimming with simulated self-righteous outrage. "You can say what you like about me and my partner here, but I'll be *damned* if I'm gonna sit here and let you deni-grate, belittle and/or malign the integrity of either Easton Westerly or Nor Westerly, who as part of one of California's foremost families are so much superior to the likes of you and me that we are not fit to lick the desert dirt off the soles of their fine Gucci footwear . . . ."

"Leafy, shut up!" interjected Beefy. "You're freaking him out. He's just kidding around, Ermine. This is what passes for a sense of humour in my partner's alternate universe. Now, if I'm not mistaken, the Westerlys own major chunks of California. So can you narrow it down just a little more?"

"With a little more time and the right resources, I think I could."

"Well," concluded Beefy, rising from his chair. "We're kinda running out of time and we really don't got too much in the way of resources. If you think of anything else, Ermine, let us know. But don't call us at police headquarters. Here, I'll give you our new secure mobile phone number."

"I won't be needing your phone number, Detective Goodness," stated the DIAPER Chief Investigating Officer with quiet determination. "That's because I'm coming with you. If you want to get up close and personal to the reptoids, you're gonna need to know their secret sign."

"If you're talking about their tails," said Leafy, "we already know about them."

"Although the reptoids may or may not possess various anatomical abnormalities like scales or tails, those aberrant attributes cannot be considered to be the secret sign. The secret sign of the Lizard People is an arbitrary, highly choreographed and statistically unlikely series of everyday movements, gestures and facial expressions that allows the reptoids and the Lizard People, of which collectively there are now millions, to definitively recognize their own kind."

"And I suppose you know this secret sign?" asked Leafy.

"Other than the Lizard People and the reptoids themselves, to the best of my knowledge there are only two untainted human beings on this planet who know what it is: myself and Doctor Hugo Fürst."

"Then why don't you save us all a lot of trouble," suggested Beefy, "and just tell us what it is."

"Because I only know the first half of the secret sign," replied Ermine Stoat. "Hugo Fürst has figured out the rest. And besides, I've devoted a goodly portion of my working life to DIAPER. The capture of a SNOTWAD is of *paramount* importance both to me and the members of my organization. If you want to infiltrate the ranks of the Lizard People, detectives, you'll have to bring me along for the ride."

Leafy and Beefy looked at each other and Beefy shrugged his indifference to the idea.

"Sure, why the hell not," acquiesced Leafy. "It's kind of like what the bible says about taking care of donkeys: before thou sniffeth thy neighbour's ass . . . take a sniff of thine own."

* * *

It was just after lunchtime and Leafy, Beefy and Ermine Stoat sat at a table in a McDonald's restaurant in downtown LA awaiting the arrival of Justin Case, Irma Manstein and Armand Hammer. The federal agent had snuck Hammer into the local FBI offices earlier that morning, allowing the super-nerd cop unfettered and unprecedented access to both the federal government's secure internal computer network and an encrypted, secret portal to the real dark web. Before leaving Carpinteria, Leafy had texted Hammer with a message that read: 'LP conference almost certainly going to happen on property owned by the Westerly family. Lol. Bill & Jerry ☺' It was sincerely hoped that this small nugget of information might be sufficient to narrow down the search for the alien's upcoming venue.

With lunch over and nothing to be done until the others arrived, Leafy decided to lighten the mood a little by telling one of the myriad 'jokes' that he had filed away in his mental library of highly dubious humour.

"Here, check this out: Four testicles, three penises, two vaginas and an asshole go into this bar for a drink and the bartender says, 'no shoes, no shirt, no service'. So one of the penises jumps up onto the bar and starts flinging beer nuts at the asshole . . . ."

"Tell me something, Detective Green," said Captain Calderon Casablancas, as he walked up unobserved behind Leafy's chair. "Do you have any other interests in that superficial, insignificant existence that you call a life besides the telling of stupid, dirty jokes?"

"You bet I do," replied Leafy unhesitatingly and without turning towards his interrogator. "Fast food, fast women and fast cars . . . but not necessarily in that order. And what's more, they don't even have to be that fast."

"To what do we owe the pleasure, Captain?" enquired Beefy. "Or are you just here for the Happy Meal special? Apparently, fifty cents from every meal goes to the Ronald McDonald luxury-cruise fund."

Triple C ignored the detectives' inane banter. For a brief moment he scrutinized Ermine Stoat as if trying to recall where he had seen him before; but did not enquire as to his identity. He turned his attention back to the detectives.

"You guys were told by the div-com — in no uncertain terms — to keep me informed about the progress of the case," said the captain, his voice brimming over with barely suppressed rage. "But just as I predicted, you've failed to do that. From this moment on, the Hollywood Sign murder is a wrap, case closed, end of story. That homicide has been solved. The gangbanger Malverde was obviously the triggerman and there is nothing left to investigate. This comes straight from the commissioner himself. You two are to move on to the next case. And believe me when I tell you, failure to comply with this order will put both your jobs and your pensions in serious jeopardy. If you guys fuck me over on this one, I promise you: I will *eat you alive*."

Triple C had said what he had come there to say and — as was his habit — was already walking away towards the exit before either detective could summon up a fitting response.

"What a pile of steaming crapola," said Leafy, as the captain left the restaurant. "With jerk-offs like him in charge, maybe it wouldn't be such a bad thing if we were taken over by the Lizard People. I feel like Triple C's scamming us somehow."

"You're damn right he is," supplied Beefy, assuredly. "Back in the Windy City we used to call it the ship-shape, shoe-shine, shilly-shally shakedown."

"Oh yeah? Well back in Oakland we used to call it the rock and roll, round-robin, red-rum rip-off."

"Is that a fact?" replied Beefy. "Well I got one word for you: deniable-plausibility. You only ever need to use it if you've inadvertently told the truth. But seriously folks, I can't help but wonder how Triple C managed to track us down to this location."

"He must have somebody tailing us, because he's way too much of a dumbass to figure out how to use an electronic tracker."

"If we've been tailed," countered Beefy, "then they're the best in the business. All I've been doing for the last couple of days is checking the rear-view mirror and I haven't spotted anything out of place."

"Okay then. If it's not a gizmo and it's not a tail," reasoned Leafy, "then somebody must have told him we were gonna be meeting here at McDonalds. I didn't tell him and you didn't tell him and Ermine didn't even know we were coming here ... so that only leaves Armand Hammer, Irma Manstein or Justin Case. My money's on the FBI agent. And I know I've said this before, Beefy, but I just don't trust that federal son of a bitch."

"Neither do I. Heads up, Leafy, here they come right now."

Hammer, Manstein and Case sat down at an adjacent table and Beefy opened the dialogue. "So, what did you find out, Armand? Don't tell me, let me guess: Elvis and Prince are alive and well and living happily ever after as test pilots for reverse-engineered flying saucers in Area 57 — which is the place that they moved everything to just before the UFO-believers stormed Area 51 — where they're protected twenty-four-seven by the men in black."

"From what I've learned today, Bill," responded Armand Hammer, with an untypically serious mien, "there are no men in black. There are, however, men in very, very dark navy blue. Unfortunately, 'men in very, very dark navy blue' is not as slick-sounding as 'men in black', so hence their popular — but sadly misconceived — designation. Incidentally, the true colour of their suits should give you a small clue as to what branch of the armed services they belong."

"So men in black kinda/sorta really exist," summed up Beefy, trying to get things straight in his head. "Except that their suits are dark blue and they're under the navy's command. Fair enough, and while that's all very interesting, Armand . . . by any chance, did you happen to find out the precise location of the ET symposium?"

"No, I didn't, Bill. But after checking out a plethora of Russian bot and troll operations on Fakebook, skimming through a dozen or so porn sites and analysing the flow of data using powerful keyword recognition software from various social media platforms including Twitter, YouTube, Snap Chat, Elite Singles, Vine, Reddit, Just Paste, Sound Cloud, Ashley Madison, Instagram, WhatsApp, Angie's List, e-Harmony, Takl, Ask.fm and Kik and then applying those results to various locations on the dark web that monitor secure government communications and population transportation algorithms, I managed to narrow down the possible location to three Westerly-owned properties. Each of these remote wilderness acreages is located within the state of California. The first is in the mountains about thirty miles north of

Twentynine Palms. The second is a few miles west of the abandoned town of Garlock at the northern edge of the Mojave Desert. And the third is slap-bang in the middle of the Mojave maybe ten miles west of the town of Baker. All the time-reference indicators point to the climax of the convention happening sometime tomorrow afternoon."

"What we need here is a good old-fashioned reconnaissance mission," suggested Irma Manstein. "With good old-fashioned human eyeballs checking out the situation in real time. Give me a chopper, a pilot, a pair of binoculars and the GPS coordinates and I'll have the exact location nailed down by suppertime."

Five pairs of eyes turned towards FBI Supervisory Special Agent Justin Case. He was the only one with the legal clout and governmental authority to arrange an extensive and expensive helicopter mission on such short notice.

"Is that doable?" asked Beefy of Case.

"Sure it's doable," conceded Justin Case, reluctantly. "It might require a magic wand, a couple of pet dragons, a unicorn's horn, a pinch of pixie dust and a shamanic faith-healer, but by and large and all things being equal, it's doable. And just for the record, who exactly is this person sitting here listening to everything we're saying?"

"That would be Ermine Stoat," answered Beefy. "Chief Investigating Officer of the Database for Inexplicable Aerial Phenomena and Extraterrestrial Research."

"Okay," said Justin Case. "So he's the CIO of DIAPER. But why is he here?"

"Because the Lizard People aint stupid," explained Leafy. "They'll sniff us out as phonies in about ten seconds flat . . . unless, of course, we show them their secret sign. Our buddy Ermine here just happens to know their secret sign — at least the first part of it — but he won't tell us what it is unless he comes with us to the reptilian reunion."

"A secret sign?" queried Armand Hammer. "You mean like the Freemason's handshake?"

"It's a bit more sophisticated than that," stated Stoat. "The secret sign of the Lizard People is an arbitrary, highly choreographed and statistically unlikely series of everyday movements, gestures and facial expressions that allows the reptoids and the Lizard People — of which collectively there are now millions — to definitively recognize their own kind."

"Ermine, I gotta hand it to you," commended Beefy. "That was word for word what you told us back in Carpinteria."

"What can I tell you?" said Stoat, smiling proudly but with a humble dignity. "I'm a precise kinda guy. Besides, I practise my spiels on a daily basis in front of the bathroom mirror right after brushing my teeth."

"If you ask me," said Justin Case. "The situational awareness of this whole affair seems to be metastasizing into a complete and uncontrollable mess . . . ."

"*Metastasizing?*" injected Leafy, with a smirk, unable to allow the word to sneak past his finely tuned affectation-monitor without mention. "Are you freaking serious?"

"All right, all right, I admit it," confessed the FBI man. "Jack Topper used it the other night on C&N and it sounded so cool and knowledgeable . . . and so yes, I've been waiting for a chance to use 'metastasizing' in everyday conversation. I don't know why, it just has a nice ring to it."

"I can't believe I'm saying this," said Manstein with a disbelieving smile, "but for once I actually agree with the skinny marine boy here. Every time somebody uses a multi-syllabic, doublespeak word like metastasizing, the person listening to it should call out the person saying the word. Or even better, just punch them right in the face. Or, if it happens to be a male, kick him in the balls. That should make them think twice about saying stupid, pretentious words so the rest of us normal-speaking people won't be subjected to any more of their pompous bull-crap."

"Roger that," agreed Leafy. "The same remedy could also be applied to people who say silly, super-trendy words like synergistic, vlogging, transmutational, nextgen, skeuomorphic, upcycling, millennial, datafication and globalization. And ditto for people who use unhyphenated, irritatingly artificial word pairings such as instructional scaffolding, disruptive innovation, fuzzy logic, herding cats, exit strategy, mission creep and buzzword compliant."

"Leafy," commented Beefy. "I didn't understand a single word you just said but that's gotta be the *smartest* thing I've ever heard you say."

"Thanks, Beefy," replied Leafy. "My mom always said that my life would have been a whole lot easier if I'd been born a whole heck of a lot smarter . . . or just a little bit stupider."

"And on that note," put in Justin Case, "Lieutenant Manstein and I have to go find a helicopter. We'll regroup later."

With a nod of farewell, Manstein got up and left with the FBI man.

"So who knows the second part of the secret sign?" asked Armand Hammer.

"None other than our tunnel-dwelling buddy, Hugo Fürst," replied Beefy. "Well, Leafy, I guess you're gonna have to once again track down the Reverend Abigail Brown so she can track down Trixie the Tagger so she can lead you through the storm drains to The Doctor and his merry band of netherworld cult-followers. And then somehow you're gonna have to try to convince him to divulge the second part of the secret sign to you."

"Even for a man of my calibre, that sounds like a mighty tall order," Leafy replied. "And what exactly are you gonna be doing while I'm negotiating with the sewer-people?"

"I thought me and Armand might go back to my place, catch a little TSN, break out some snacks and maybe suck back on a couple of cold ones. Take Ermine with you. He's Hugo Fürst's good buddy and maybe The Doctor will listen to him. You guys give us a call when you've got things sorted out. And one more thing, Leafy . . . we *definitely* don't need anybody else joining us on our little 'alien intervention'. We've got way too many bodies as it is."

CHAPTER EIGHT

Deus Ex Machina

With a total of thirty-three sentient beings on board — twenty-three humans, four spiders, three houseflies, two mice and one reptoid — the school bus rumbled eastward along Interstate 15 at its top speed of forty-seven miles per hour into the heart of the Mojave Desert. The bus belonged to the Last Chance Mission and was normally used to transport members of the Reverend Abigail Brown's homeless flock on day excursions away from the harsh realities of Skid Row. But today, which was, quite fittingly, the Sabbath, the old yellow vehicle was being utilized for a very different purpose — a grand and noble purpose — as the advance guard of the counter-offensive against the encroaching ranks of an invading alien race and their genetically altered human followers. With its exterior decked out with Christian symbols and various quotes from scripture, the bus was perfectly camouflaged for the job in hand. Irma Manstein and Justin Case had returned from their helicopter journey with the news that the alien conference was being held in the desert not far from the town of Baker and that the cover story for the event was that it was nothing more than a gathering of born-again Christians getting together to commune with their God.

Behind the wheel of the bus sat Jimmy One-Thumb, the Reverend Brown's Navajo driver and go-to guy to fulfil such diverse responsibilities as building maintenance person, short-order cook and personal bodyguard. Jimmy was an ex-con who had — metaphorically speaking —finally seen the Lord. He was a big, muscular guy in his early thirties who claimed to have lost his right thumb in a fight to the death with a mountain lion in the Sierras. But the truth was somewhat more mundane, having injured the digit on a building site in San Diego when a fellow construction worker had accidentally dropped a concrete block on his right hand, causing the thumb to become irreparably infected and thus requiring amputation. The Reverend Brown had helped and guided Jimmy One-Thumb through various bouts of homelessness, alcoholism and drug addiction, and in return he was now entirely devoted to the iron-haired preacher as her slightly incomplete right-hand man. Preoccupied with driving the bus, Jimmy quietly sung one of his favourite tunes.

"The Donald inside, the Donald inside . . . Every single one of us, the Donald inside."

Standing in the aisle behind Jimmy One-Thumb, Hugo Fürst was now taking his turn — after Ermine Stoat's presentation of the first part — to teach the human passengers the finer points of the second part of the secret sign. And like Ermine Stoat, both Hugo Fürst and the Reverend Brown had refused to cooperate with the detectives unless they too could come along to the reptoid reunion. And while the Reverend had chosen to bring only her driver, Hugo Fürst had brought along several of his young graffiti-painting followers, including Trixie the Tagger.

"Nein, nein, nein!" admonished Fürst, momentarily reverting in exasperation to his native Austrian tongue. "You scratch your left earlobe with your right forefinger . . . while simultaneously lifting your left foot and rotating it in a clockwise direction. Like so."

Hugo Fürst was impatient and by no means a good teacher, but his physical dexterity was impressive, allowing him to demonstrate the movements in a fairly clear fashion, and all but Leafy seemed to be getting the hang of it.

"Detective Green!" commanded Fürst, pointing an imperious finger that looked not unlike an old-school Nazi Gruppenführer's stiff salute. "Get to the back of the bus! You are not only physically incompetent, you are quite obviously choreographically challenged and you are throwing everybody off their stride."

The school bus was not equipped with an air conditioner, and despite the fact that every window that could open had been opened and that, quite ironically, the temperature in the desert was lower than in the city, the bus was still, in effect, a glass and metal sweatbox. Humbly and obediently, Leafy took a seat at the back of the bus, wiped the perspiration from his brow and was overtaken by a tremendous sense of déjà vu. This could be his first day in kindergarten or his last day in the Marines, or any of many days that had occurred in between. He felt that, in one way or another, he had always been out of sync with the rest of humanity and always looking for a place where he could truly fit in. In his heart of hearts, he knew that without Beefy's friendship, he would have long since left the police force and moved on to God knows where doing God knows what. For whatever reason, his mind turned to the blonde-haired, blue-leotarded, dog-walking, joke-telling, muscle-car-loving roller-blade lady that had given them the information that had ultimately led to Malverde. He now wished that he had had the presence of mind to get her name and phone number, and he made a mental note to make a serious effort to track her down and hopefully get to know her a little better. Maybe he would borrow Tucker the lie-sniffing dog to bolster his avowed love for the canine species. It surely wouldn't hurt.

Leafy lit a cigarette and watched from the back as Irma Manstein, Justin Case, Armand Hammer, Ermine Stoat, Beefy Goodness, the

Reverend Abigail Brown, Trixie the Tagger and all of her streetwise buddies attempted to emulate — with varying degrees of success, but all of them *way* better than Leafy — the second part of the secret sign as revealed by Doctor Hugo Fürst.

"At this point," continued Fürst. "You must raise your eyebrows like this as though suddenly surprised, take a very deep breath, exhale and then turn your head ninety degrees to the right, while scratching your left buttock with the two middle fingers of your left hand. To conclude the secret sign, you must take one step forward with your right foot, tap the top of your head with the palm of your left hand, take a yawn and leave your mouth wide open, flick your tongue quickly in and out of your mouth three times like so and then extend your right hand as though to shake hands with whomever you are interacting. But at the very last moment, you retract your hand, place your right thumb against the tip of your nose and waggle your fingers in a random fashion. You then smile mischievously for approximately seven seconds, take a short bow and exit stage right. And that, ladies and gentlemen, is *The Secret Sign of the Lizard People*."

The previous night, after considering the ramifications of Triple C's tirade, Leafy and Beefy had agreed that today's excursion would not and could not be classified as official police business and that no matter what happened, they would be acting purely as private citizens. And as such, they had left their service weapons at home. When Monday morning rolled around, they would dutifully and obediently pick up the next homicide file on the top of the pile and do their very best to forget all about the N. Emma Johnson case.

Having quickly and easily learnt the moves of the secret sign, Beefy went to the 'bad boy's section' at the back of the bus to see how his recalcitrant partner was doing. Leafy looked forlorn and Beefy searched his mind for something to say that might cheer him up.

"When your time comes, which would be your preference?" enquired Beefy, solicitously. "Cremation or burial?"

"Neither," replied Leafy. "I was considering cryogenics, but I hear it's quite expensive. Plus, I don't really like the cold."

"Just like you were saying about Keef Richass, there are a couple of funeral facilitators — they don't call themselves undertakers anymore — that do burials at sea. With you having been one of Uncle Sam's Misguided Children, an ex-navy man and all . . . ."

"Nah, I don't think so. I get seasick just looking at a boat."

"Fair enough. We'll cross fish food off the list. But at this point, you're kinda running out of funereal options, though."

"Funereal? Do you realize that's fun and real with an 'E' in between? Are you sure that's even a bona fide word, Beefy?"

"Surprisingly enough, I'm fairly certain it is a bona fide word. At least that's what my mom told me. I guess it's all about trying to reach a higher plane."

"What do mean? Like an SR 71 Blackbird or a U2?"

"Plane of existence, Leafy."

"Right, right, right. It's too bad that that English guy's 'space flight for the common man' thing hasn't really taken off. What was his name? Sir Roger Brainstorm? Something like that. Anyhow, I think sending your lifeless body up into outer space would be a totally cool grand finale."

"I agree. But even if Sir Whatever His Name Is' ever does get his act together, the whole thing was never really designed for the common man, and it's probably way beyond the financial scope of the funereal clause in your police department insurance policy."

"Yeah, you're probably right. But now that you've got me thinking about it, what I'd really like to do when the time comes — assuming I've still got the strength to do it — is climb up one of those big old redwood trees . . . ."

"But you don't like heights, Leafy."

"True. But I wouldn't have to climb to the very top. Somewhere in the middle would do. If you picked the right tree, nobody would ever find you up there. They say that each mature redwood is a whole separate eco-system in its own right. Anyhow, I'd find me a nice, big fat branch to lie down on, tie myself down so I don't fall off, maybe sink a few shots of seven-year-old bourbon, take a last look at that big old blue sky and then . . . make good and final use of my trusty police-issue sidearm."

"The Remington Retirement Plan? Really?"

"Sure, why not? Hidden away up in one of those giant redwoods would be the only way for a man to ensure that his body is being disposed of in a natural and respectful fashion and not being sold off on the dark web for spare parts to some vodka-guzzling Russian oligarch with a worn-out liver."

"So it would be kind of like . . . your very last act of self-determination?"

"Precisely."

"I like that. It's got Leafy Green written all over it."

"'Do not flow mental into that mud fight,'" misquoted Leafy. "'Rave, rave against the flying of the kite.'"

"'Really? I thought it was: 'Do not thwow fent'nyl into that Bud Lite™. Wage, wage against the fwying of the twite.' FYI: that's how posh, poetry-loving Brits with a rhotacistic bent pronounce the word trout."

"Yeah. Maybe so. But I think that line comes a lot later in the verse."

"All I can say is that those old-school Welsh bards sure knew how to pen a piercing and profitable poem. And before you say anything else," said Beefy, holding up a restraining hand, "I'm entirely aware that bards is just bastards without the 'STA' in the middle. It's just like that popular idiom: 'There's too many poets and not enough prostitutes in this world.'"

"No, no," corrected Leafy. "It's: 'There's plenty of pros and not enough destitutes in this world.'"

"I'm pretty sure poets was in there somewhere."

"Okay then: 'There's plenty of pros and not enough doets in this world.' FYI: that's a compound word with destitutes and poets combined."

"Because poetitutes doesn't sound quite right. Right?"

"Right," acknowledged Leafy. "It's a good thing MS Word™ has that 'add to dictionary' function or we'd have squiggly red lines all over the place right now. So tell me, Beefy, what does the pros/doets saying really mean?"

"Well . . . it speaks to the primal urges that have come to dominate the psyche of the twenty-first century emotionally-deprived male as he slowly progresses — mechanically and meaninglessly — through the obligatory way-posts of a technologically-driven life, malcontented and yet culturally concave, while at the same time desperately struggling to comprehend the ominously dysfunctional sentiments inherent within the strange socio-political dichotomy . . . ."

"Strange socio-political dichotomy? Please! That's one step beyond cool, Beefy. In fact, that's a fridge too far."

"A fridge too far? Maybe so . . . but not all dichotomies are perfectly straight forward, you know. There is on occasion such a thing as a strange dichotomy. Which in turn, could very easily turn out to be of the socio-political variety. Really. It could happen."

"You don't have the faintest clue what that pros/doets expression means, do you?" asked Leafy.

"Nope," admitted Beefy, with a sheepish grin. "And what's more, I don't think I ever will."

"I'm glad we sorted that out."

"Me too."

"You know, Beefy," stated Leafy, with a slightly worried look. "My main problem right now is that I'll never get the hang of that damned secret sign."

"I know. Your talents lie in a completely different sector of human activity."

"If it comes up, I'll just have to explain to the reptoids that I've never been any good at learning that sort of stuff. I'm not a rhythmically graceful person. It's just like you and 'you go first with an omelette' so rightly pointed out: I'm choreographically challenged. And besides, it probably doesn't even matter if I get the hang of it or not. Because if

Justin Case is really the sneaky little rat we think he is then the aliens already know we're on our way."

"We'll figure it out when the time comes. Don't sweat the small stuff, man."

"I've tried sweating both the medium and the large stuff, but for whatever reason, they just don't sweat right with me. Every time I start building up a sweat about them, all the small stuff comes rushing right back in to be re-sweated alongside the un-sweated medium and large stuff."

"I hear you, bro. Sweating stuff — small, medium or large — can be an excruciatingly frustrating way to pass the time."

"Listen, Beefy," spoke Leafy in a low voice shaded with melancholy. "If we don't make it out of this thing alive . . . there's something I've been meaning to ask you for a very long time, old buddy."

"Hit me with it, sailor."

"Why are bodily fluids usually depicted with the colour blue in feminine-hygiene commercials?"

"That's a no-brainer," responded Beefy, with alacrity. "It's because — unlike spiders — we don't have any bodily fluids that are coloured blue. Green has connotations of snot, phlegm and mucus — or, as we used to say in the army: snophus. Anything reddish immediately brings to mind blood. Yellow obviously makes you think of pee. And we all know what brown means. The advertisers use blue as a sort of colour euphemism to get their marketing point across without causing undue offence to Joan Public. They want her to *buy* the product, not vomit all over her favourite Lazy Girl recliner. Unless, of course, the ad is for Lazy Girl recliners. In which case, they probably *do* want her to vomit all over it, thus obviating the necessity for any form of built-in accelerated obsolescence mechanism to be included in the initial stages of product manufacture."

"You've really put some thought into this," Leafy commended. "I'm really quite stupefied."

"Stupefied?"

"Enthralled, mesmerised, captivated."

"Let's just settle for rapt or gript. Okay?"

"Okay."

At the front of the school bus, Irma Manstein stepped up beside Jimmy One-Thumb and began to issue the final driving directions.

"Arrowhead Trail should be the next interchange, Jimmy. Here we go."

Jimmy took the off-ramp and came to a stop at the tee-junction beside the interstate.

"Okay," said Manstein, as she checked out her old-school road map. "Turn left and head under the freeway bridge onto Zzyzx Road."

"Zzyzx Road?" queried One-Thumb. "What the heck kind of name for a road is that?"

"That's a totally, wildly weird name for a road," replied Manstein. "But there it is on the map, so keep following it north towards those mountains."

"There actually used to be some kind of resort out here," remarked Justin Case, having earlier researched the place online. "Some religious nut built it back at the end of WWII way out here in the middle of nowhere. To get a little peace and quiet, I guess. The abandoned buildings should be coming up pretty soon."

The terrain beside Zzyzx Road was as flat as a proverbial pancake, and the salt and soda flats that stretched off into the distance on either side looked mercilessly dry and hugely inhospitable. For long stretches of the road, the desert winds had blown the fine, powdery sand over the blacktop and clouds of reddish dust spewed out from behind the bus as it proceeded due north. Before they had covered even a quarter of a mile, they were joined overhead by an eight-rotor drone very similar to the one Manstein, Leafy and Beefy had encountered in the Gang Unit car park.

"Heads up," said Manstein as she focussed her binoculars on the dark flying machine. "We've got company up above. Same deal as last time, but this time without the weapon."

"It looks like we've got company to the rear as well," noted Leafy as he tried to peer through the curtain of dust at a vehicle that was following a few hundred yards behind them.

They were now irreversibly committed, and an unspoken ripple of apprehension permeated throughout the occupants of the bus as the reality of their quest finally sunk in and they drew ever closer to their destination. Up ahead in the near distance in a wide valley between the mountains, a small city of tents, RVs, concession stands, communication trailers and what looked like a huge stage shared the desert landscape with a ramshackle assortment of derelict buildings and structures. Incongruously, a fair-sized lake seemed to appear out of nowhere, its shores surrounded by towering Royal Palms that had been festooned with bright religious banners. At the very centre of the gathering stood a large, dome-shaped object that had been painstakingly covered over with a multi-coloured patchwork of tarpaulins, perhaps to protect whatever it was from the desert environment or perhaps to hide it from prying eyes.

"Do I have a problem believing in these Lizard People?" asked Jimmy One-Thumb, who had an irksome tendency to occasionally lapse into unprompted phases of asked and answered self-interrogation. "I have no problem believing in them. It's well known amongst my tribe that the ancient 'Star-People' were reptiles. Do I think that the Star-People have returned? You bet I do. Do I think they are going to kick our asses? I can't think of a single reason why they wouldn't."

"Pipe down, Jimmy," commanded the Reverend Brown. "That sort of un-Christian defeatist talk is no help to anybody. Never forget that we have God on our side and that He will *never* allow these otherworldly pagan parasites to triumph over the true and rightful inhabitants of this world."

"Yes ma'am," responded Jimmy, with an unconvinced shake of his head, "and I sure hope you're right about that."

As the bus neared the perimeter of the gathering, Supervisory Special Agent Justin Case stood up at the front of the vehicle and held up a quieting hand.

"Listen up, people. Our primary goal here today is to gather indisputable evidence of the aliens' existence that can be presented to the outside world at large. I was going to suggest that you upload any photos you take directly onto the Cloud in real time . . . but my phone is indicating zero bars of reception. Has anybody got any cell reception?"

A panicked hubbub took place as everybody checked their phones, but the FBI man's query was greeted with an uneasy negative silence.

"Okay," continued Case. "It looks like they chose this place not just because of its remoteness, but because it also happens to be an RFSSDZ. FYI: that's a 'radio frequency signal strength dead zone' to the uninitiated. No one ever said the Lizard People were stupid. All I can say is try to be as discreet as you can if you're taking pictures or collecting any items of interest. Which brings me to our secondary goal. And this is where things might get a little gnarly, if not downright sketchy. If at all possible, we want to capture one of these creatures — a SNOTWAD, as Mr. Stoat calls them, a *real* lizard person — and then return with it to civilisation for the whole world to see. So at this point, I'll turn you over to Lieutenant Manstein. She's in charge of this part of the operation and also in charge of getting us all out of here in one piece."

Irma Manstein stood up and, in her inimitable fashion, briefed the passengers on this part of the mission.

"Once we're inside the perimeter we'll split up into groups of two to conduct a surreptitious search of the site. The school bus will be our base of operations, and that's where I'll be. If you find the aliens or you get into any kind of trouble, just make your way back to the bus and I'll deal with it."

Jimmy One-Thumb brought the bus to a squeaking halt beside a makeshift security checkpoint that spanned the width of Zzyzx Road. He opened the doors and the Reverend Abigail Brown stepped out to talk to the two young men who manned the checkpoint. They both wore matching fluorescent-orange reflective vests with the word 'STAFF' printed on the chest and the phrase 'Come to Jesus' on the back. They smiled respectfully at the reverend as she explained who she was and what she represented. Now that the dust had settled, it could be clearly seen that the vehicle behind the bus was not a mirror-windowed, armour-plated SUV stuffed with heavily armed men in very, very dark navy blue suits, but a young, clean-cut family in a minivan with a Jesus-fish sticker on the windshield. If you discounted the searing heat, it was actually a beautiful day in the desert with clear skies for as far as the eye could see, the deep-azure blue streaked with the contrails of high-flying jetliners making their way to and from Los Angeles International Airport. After about thirty seconds the reverend stepped back on board with a mirthless, yet triumphant smile.

"Close the doors, Jimmy," she said. "We're good to go. Now just follow the green arrow signs for the campgrounds."

"Didn't they ask to see the secret sign, Reverend?" queried Justin Case.

"They made no mention of the secret sign," replied the reverend.

"Don't worry," Hugo Fürst piped up, ominously. "Sooner or later — mark my words — the Secret Sign of the Lizard People is going to come up."

* * *

The reptoids had done such a magnificent job of covering up their operation that both Beefy and Leafy still harboured some tiny niggling doubts as to the reality of the alien conference. For all intents and purposes, the two police officers were presently strolling through a harmless Christian encampment of believers with no indications of anything strange or untoward. For this very reason, the two had decided that right off the bat they would investigate the only suspicious thing to have presented itself thus far: the domed object that lay concealed beneath the tarpaulins. To avoid revealing their true purpose, Leafy and Beefy meandered their way indirectly via a circuitous route in the general direction of the object.

"So what do you think it is hidden under those covers?" asked Beefy, keeping his voice at a discreet volume.

"What do I think it is? I think it's a flying freaking saucer under those covers."

"All right," allowed Beefy. "Let's assume, just for the sake of argument, mind you, that it is an alien spaceship. What the heck are we supposed to do about it?"

"Well . . . I guess we'd better take some pictures of it before it rises like a penis from the ashes."

"Phoenix."

"Say what?"

"Rises like a *phoenix* from the ashes," clarified Beefy. "You said penis."

"Phoenix? How can the largest city in Arizona rise? That doesn't even make a lick of sense, Beefy."

"Then you explain to me how a penis makes sense."

"Well, heck, everybody knows that penises rise. That's what they do. They rise to the occasion. They rise of their own accord. Some penises are late risers, some penises are early risers, but just about all of them eventually rise to the challenge. If they didn't rise there'd be no human race. The same thing applies to animals. So there you have it, Leafy's magic philosophical formula: no rising penises equals no people and no animals. I admit, it doesn't paint much of a pretty picture, but I believe it adequately and eloquently explains my point."

"Then how does the *ashes* bit fit in with your penis proverb?"

"That . . . I don't know. I have to admit that the ashes bit has always been a bit of a puzzle to me. Unless they're talking about a botched cremation or something . . . ."

"Yeah, I don't get it either," sighed Beefy. "Ashes doesn't even make sense when you put it with Phoenix. Unless they're talking about a nuclear war or a really big fire in the city centre or something . . . ."

"Who the hell knows?"

They were now within fifty feet of the veiled domed object and they could plainly see that multiple reels of razor wire had been uncoiled on the ground around its circumference, effectively fencing off the object from its surroundings. Several men wearing reflective 'STAFF' vests stood nonchalantly around the perimeter, making it virtually impossible to approach the object in broad daylight without being detected.

"Oh well," said Beefy. "So much for that idea. What's next on our to-do list?"

"As far as I recall, Beefy, that's all that was on the list. I did happen to notice that one of those parked trailers on the way to the camping area happened to be a Binder Dundat's Spicy Hot Asian Yummy Delectables concession stand. Maybe we should grab an early lunch. What do you think?"

"I think that's a mighty fine idea. I've been meaning to try some of that Indian curry cuisine for quite a while now . . . ."

At that moment, a ringing sound emanated from the public address loudspeakers that had been set up here and there around the venue, signalling that an announcement was about to be made.

"Hello everybody and welcome," said the voice from the loudspeakers. "Our spokespersons and special guests are about to take to the stage. Please make your way to the audience-participation area in front of the stage to hear their message and bear witness to the truth. Thank you."

Leafy and Beefy were not that far from the stage, and they made their way with everybody else to the wide-open space specified in the announcement. As the crowd got bigger and bigger, sound engineers and lighting technicians made their last-minute tweaks to the electronic equipment up on stage. An air of anticipation rippled through the spectators, lending to the proceedings the feel of a rock concert or perhaps a political rally. The huge video screen, which towered some fifty feet above the stage, burst into life offering a stunningly high-definition close-up view of the stage below.

Behind the stage a white marquee had been erected and, as the opening bars of the 'Star Spangled Banner' rang out from the loudspeakers, the spokespersons began to emerge one by one, forming a line across the front of the dais. Many of them were immediately recognizable, an eclectic Clintonesque basket of deplorables that included billionaires, celebrities, politicians, social luminaries, NASCAR drivers, rodeo riders, masters of industry, public servants, red-necked white-supremacists, white-necked orange-supremacists, Big John-loving ranch owners, Charlatan Hesten's exhumed zombified corpse and — even though it was still some months before Yuletide — a Victorian-attired entity that appeared to be the Ghost of Christmas Past. Most notable to Leafy and Beefy were the LAPD commissioner, the mayor of Los Angeles and Binder Dundat. As the national anthem came to a close, a tall, reddish-haired woman stepped up to the podium and addressed the crowd. It was none other than Nor Westerly, Easton Westerly's daughter and heir apparent to the vast Westerly business empire. She was dressed in a form-fitting, pink and grey designer jogging suit, her expertly arranged hair and professionally applied make-up softening the somewhat angular cut of her facial features and the bleak coldness of her eyes.

"Ladies and gentlemen, sisters and brothers," her words rang out, in a voice accustomed to being listened to within the inner circles of power. She made a slight adjustment to her headset mic and then continued with her address. "We have all made the pilgrimage here today for one reason and one reason only: to establish and celebrate the impending New World Order. Much has been made of the word democracy in this country. It is a word that was never actually mentioned by the founding fathers nor was it included in the Constitution and yet . . . 'democracy' is bandied around as though it is a magic remedy for this entire nation's — or for that matter, the entire world's — problems. Well, I for one refuse to genuflect before the altar of unfettered egalitarianism. Those of us in the know realize that America has never been a true democracy and that we are in fact an out-and-out, no-messing-around *plutocracy*. Every president in our history has been bought and paid for and comes to office with a huge list of political favours that have to be repaid to his financiers over the full term of his office. To a lesser extent, the same applies to the so-called democracies of our western allies. Only the ancient Greeks have ever come close to the tenets of a true democracy, but even they were prone to what I regard to be the three natural default settings of the human race: greed, excess and corruption. Of course, those of us in the know have no problem with the nation being controlled by the rich elite, but what we do have a problem with is the hypocrisy of pretending otherwise. Very shortly, there will no longer be a need for such a pretence. *You*, my sisters and brothers, are the chosen ones. *You* are the elite. And together we will rule this nation and this planet as the true custodians of the New World Order. Now before I introduce you to our *extra-special* guests from afar, let us all join together in TSSOTLP."

After a rousing bout of cheering and applause had subsided, Nor Westerly — not unlike some virally-popular, keep-fit, lose-weight, mega-guru on YouTube — led the crowd and those onstage through the opening movements of the Secret Sign of the Lizard People.

"It is my sad duty to tell you all," continued Nor Westerly, talking into her tiny headset mic while unerringly performing the ritual complexities of the secret sign, "that even as I speak, there are those amongst us who do not belong. Look around you and weed out the intruders. They are not hard to spot. In fact, there's one right there in front of me."

Up above on the big silver screen, Nor Westerly's bejewelled right forefinger pointed like a sniper rifle directly at the epicentre of Detective Jerome Green's heart.

* * *

It was now late in the afternoon and the desert sun beat mercilessly down upon the heads of the twenty people held captive within the fenced compound. Leafy and Beefy's suspicions about a traitor in their midst had unfortunately turned out to be all too true, and one by one, the passengers of the school bus had been methodically rounded up and imprisoned inside the makeshift jail. The only ones that had not yet been caught were Irma Manstein, Armand Hammer and Justin Case.

Manstein had stashed a small armoury of weapons on the bus and if necessary, had been prepared to fight her way out of here if things had gone wrong. Things had most definitely gone wrong and about an hour ago several volleys of automatic gunfire had rung out across the desert sands, and Leafy and Beefy feared that Manstein and possibly Armand Hammer as well had gone down in a final blaze of glory. The two detectives were under no illusions about their predicament and they realized that they and the rest of their fellow captives were now in the direst of dire straits.

"You got any regrets, Leafy?" asked Beefy.

"Regrets?"

"You know . . . mistakes that you've made, things that you would've liked to have put right in your life."

"Holy shit, man!" replied Leafy with a poignant grin. "I make more mistakes before breakfast than most people make in a month. On that basis I'd be spending my whole life in a permanent state of regret."

"My biggest regret right now is that I didn't kiss the wife goodbye this morning. She likes to sleep in on weekends so I didn't have the heart to wake her up. But I *did* pat the dog."

"Well, at least that's something. You know, Beefy, aside from Prince Andrew — the seven-legged pet tarantula I had when I was a kid — you're the best friend I ever had . . . but I can't help but think that you're missing out on something pretty important here. Just think of all the lessons you've learnt and the fun that you've had making all of those mistakes. There's no sense in regretting them now. Those mistakes have made you the person that you are. That's what life is all about. The whole thing is just a huge learning-curve and who really cares if you occasionally drop the ball? We're all just winging it anyway. I mean, what don't you get about the phrase: 'To err is human'? Once you accept that simple premise . . . man, let me tell ya, it takes a whole load of weight off a person's shoulders."

Before Beefy could respond, a ruckus from outside the fence drew everybody's attention. It was Captain Calderon Casablancas and a group of people that Leafy and Beefy recognized as being fellow LAPD officers. They were all armed, but none of them were in police uniform and between them they carried a semi-conscious man in a dark-grey suit. They unlocked the gate and unceremoniously dumped him on the ground inside the compound. The man's face was bruised and battered but clearly identifiable as that of FBI Supervisory Special Agent Justin Case.

"That's a hell of a way to thank your undercover guy, Captain," observed Leafy. "Is that how you reptoids treat your buddies?"

"Green," responded Triple C with a #superscasty smile. "You are *such* an idiot. He's not the spy, you jackass. It's super-nerd Armand Hammer who stabbed you guys in the back. Oh, and by the way, your lesbian friend Lieutenant Man-face tried to play the hero . . . but unfortunately for her, she suddenly reached her expiration date."

In the near distance, a rousing chorus of cheers exploded from the reptoids around the stage area and from beneath the concealment of its covers the Lizard People's silver, dome-shaped craft began to noiselessly ascend into the sky.

"Do you remember the warning I gave to you guys yesterday back at McDonalds?" asked Triple C. "Let me refresh your memories. I told you to back off or I would eat you alive. Well, guess what time it is right now? It's *dinner time*. And you two are the first course."

Triple C gestured to his henchmen to grab Leafy and Beefy, but before they could carry out his unspoken command, Ermine Stoat stepped forward between the detectives and their captors. His long dark hair hung down around his shoulders and in that moment, as a beam of pure white sunlight reflected off the spacecraft and illuminated the crown of his head, he had never looked more messianic.

"Before you do anything totally foolish, Captain," advised Stoat. "You would be wise to remember the inherent perils for somebody of your ilk with regard to the principle of *Deus ex Machina*."

"Day you sex my sheen her?" asked Triple C. "What kinda peace-and-kindness, magic-mushroom trash-talk is that, hippie-boy?"

"*Deus . . . ex . . . Machina*," elucidated Stoat, as if to an infant. "An unforeseen and fortuitous event — usually involving a sympathetic divine being descending from the sky upon some form of mechanical apparatus — that brings about a happy conclusion when the protagonists have seemingly exhausted all hope of escaping their perilous circumstances."

And high in the sky above, some fluffy white clouds appeared in the otherwise clear-blue skies and a millisecond later, the alien spaceship disintegrated into a billion particles of matter and light, destroyed beyond any hope of salvation. The fluffy white clouds parted and the Judeo-Christian-God gracefully descended from the heavens upon a triangular golden chariot. The people down below knew that it was the Judeo-Christian-God because a huge white banner hung below the golden chariot, and written in both Hebrew and English were the words: 'Behold the Judeo-Christian-God'. Triple C and the rest of the Lizard People's human followers cowered in fear, as they sensed that the time of their come-uppance was close at hand.

As the triangular golden chariot touched down gently upon the ground it could be seen that the JCG — who happened to bear an uncanny resemblance to Kneel Yonge, but perhaps not quite as self-righteous looking — was accompanied by three angels, one at each corner of the chariot. Interestingly, the JCG was not dressed in his trademark robes, but had instead chosen for this particular occasion a fringed and colourfully beaded deerskin Native American outfit with a single white eagle feather hanging down from his long, grey hair. For his age, He looked really good. The angels were also familiar looking and also looked really good. The first bore an uncanny resemblance to Tailor Shift; the second an uncanny resemblance to Katie Penny; and the third an uncanny resemblance to Mylie Sirens. It was hard to imagine this particular threesome in such close spiritual proximity, but as they crooned a heavily auto-tuned angelic chorus of oohs and aahs in the background, it made for a most inspiring moment. As was his wont, the JCG came straight to the point.

"Very shortly, my angels and I are going to smite the invading aliens' tainted human followers and balance will once again be restored to the planet Earth. As for you untainted people, I suggest that you get outta here before the smiting process begins. Oh, and JSYK . . . ."

"Just so you know," interpreted the Tailor Shift look-alike angel, with an ethereal smile.

"Including Earth," the JCG went on, "there are seventeen hundred and sixty-seven inhabited planets in this galaxy and a goodly chunk of them fall under my jurisdiction. So it goes without saying that I'm a very busy God with a wicked crazy schedule and, despite all of the rumours to the contrary, the pesky and immutable laws of physics preclude me from being in two places at one time. So while I might occasionally be a little tardy in dealing with your problems, have faith that I will always turn up eventually. Now, like I said, you people get outta here, and no matter what happens, for God's sake . . . do *not* look back."

Ermine Stoat stepped forward, and for several blessed moments, locked eyes with one of the most laid-back deities in the Milky Way Galaxy. The JCG nodded his approval and gestured for Ermine to take his rightful place beside Him in the golden chariot; but Ermine rejected the tempting offer with a silent shake of his head. The JCG shrugged his broad shoulders in a gesture of vague disappointment, but as always, signed off with a confident smile and an informal salute.

"Praise be to the JCG," sang the beautiful angels, in perfect harmony, over and over again, as the golden chariot slowly ascended to a safe smiting altitude where they waited patiently for the untainted humans to get clear of the soon-to-be-smitten area.

* * *

The reptoids that had attended the alien conference had been so secretive about their plans that their friends, family and close associates did not connect their disappearance with the strange and calamitous event that had occurred in the desert. The *Los Angeles Times* had run a banner headline on the Monday morning which read: 'GIANT METEOR CRATER APPEARS IN THE MOJAVE — SCIENTISTS ARE LOOKING INTO IT'. But like most front-page news, the public's monkey-short attention span — and that's probably, if not assuredly, an insult to monkeys — had quickly relegated it to the newspaper's middle sections and then forgotten within the week.

It was now over twelve months after the fact, and the body-less funeral service for Lieutenant Irma Manstein, who had by now been officially classified as deceased, had just come to a close. A total of seventeen sentient beings had attended the short ceremony at the funeral facilitation centre, a list that included: the Reverend Abigail Brown, Jimmy One-Thumb, Manstein's one-time live-in girlfriend, Manstein's mother, two of Manstein's colleagues from the Gang Unit, Detective Sergeant William Goodness, Detective Jerome Green, the funeral facilitator, the funeral facilitator's helper, four insects of three different species, two spiders and a baby scorpion. Perhaps unsurprisingly, the service had been a sad and dismal affair, and Leafy and Beefy were glad to be sitting once again in the air-conditioned comfort of their Crown Victoria. Despite the patently absurd and vehement denials from the alt-right about the very existence of global-warming, the recurrence of yet another record-breaking Californian heat wave was really no great shocker to anybody in the state. In an effort to stay cool, both detectives sucked contentedly through their drinking-straws from super-sized, real-fruit slushies.

"I worshipped the ground that woman walked on," stated Leafy, between slurps.

"If you're talking about Irma — and I'm pretty sure you are — she hated your guts and she also scared the bejesus out of you."

"There was a certain element of trepidation — mostly on my part — in our relationship, I'll grant you that . . . but I didn't let that stop me from loving her."

"Loving her?" parroted Beefy with a disbelieving smile.

"All right, I liked her a lot. An *awful* lot."

"No you didn't. What the hell is wrong with you? Why don't you just be honest?"

"Because you're not supposed to speak ill of the dead."

"Then just don't say anything," suggested Beefy. "Or say something positive but inoffensive like: 'Irma was very proud of her Teutonic heritage.'"

"Why would she proud of that, for pity's sake? What have the Germans ever given us besides two world wars, more efficient gas ovens, the original ICBMs and the measles?"

"All right, I admit," admitted Beefy. "That was not the best example I could have come up with, but I think you catch my drift."

"All this talk about Germans puts me in mind of dictators."

"What about them?"

"Who's your all-time favourite dictator?" quizzed Leafy, genuinely interested in hearing his partner's response.

"Oh man, that's a tough one. There's been so many good ones. For sheer arrogance, Mussolini, Gaddafi or Idi Amin spring to mind, but for all-around, no-messing about dictatorishness . . . ."

"Dictatorability," corrected Leafy, obligingly.

". . . Dictatorability, I think it comes down to two guys: Chairman Mau or Uncle Joe. Both of them managed to kill millions more than Hitler ever did and both managed to stay in power for a very long time. But if I had to choose between the Chinese guy and the Russian, I think the moustache would have to take the prize. There's nothing worse than a clean-shaven dictator."

"Facial hair definitely adds a certain . . . thuggish charm to a man's face. Or — for the sake of political correctness — thuggish charm to a woman's face. I know this much: They don't make 'em like they used to, Beefy."

"That's for sure, Leafy. And now, just for a refreshing change, I got a stupid question for you: Who's your all-time favourite bible character?"

"Old Testament or New?"

"Old."

"The beginning, the middle or the end?"

"The end."

AFTERWORD

There are many reasons for taking on the responsibility of writing a book.

For me, three simultaneous — yet seemingly unrelated — occurrences converged to inspire me to create this book.

Firstly, the alarming resurgence of global right-wing populism to a level not seen since before the Second World War. (There is a conspiracy here, folks, but it's definitely not a theory.)

Secondly, the immense power and wealth wielded by the giant corporations and their cynical denial of the on-going industrial-scale destruction of our planet's flora and fauna despite an overabundance of scientific evidence to the contrary.

And lastly, but by no means leastly, the huge popularity of the UFO counter-culture and the resultant conspiracy theories that now resonate throughout our literature and social media.

The absolute evil of the first two and the arguably harmless absurdity of the last proved such an irresistibly interesting combination, that I had no choice but to tie these themes together and *The Secret Sign of the Lizard People* came into being.

Dark political metaphor or raucous irreverent spoof . . . or some strange mixed-up, messed-up creature in between? Due to subject proximity, I personally cannot say. So I'll leave it to you, my perceptive reader, to make that determination through your eyes as the beholder.

Sláinte!
Kevin E. Buckley

ABOUT THE AUTHOR

Born in the United Kingdom but happily dwelling "across the pond", Kevin E. Buckley has travelled far and wide seeking new experiences and delving into interesting cultures. His travels ultimately led him to the pristine wilderness of the Great White North, the perfect setting for him to freely express his creativity. When not putting pencil to paper, Kevin is a business owner and musician and has played lead guitar with various rock and blues acts in both the Old World and the New. Choreographically challenged from an early age, he has fought hard to overcome a seriously debilitating dancing disability. On the plus side, he is now widely recognized as a fully-fledged, genetically-certified non-reptoid. *The Secret Sign of the Lizard People* is Kevin's first published work.

www.kevinebuckley.com

Nutrition Facts

8 servings per volume

Serving size   **1 Chapter**

Amount Per Serving

Calories   **0**

	% Daily Value*
Total Fact 3.2g	**0.6%**
Saturated Fact 0g	
Trans Fact 0g	
Polyunsaturated Fiction 249.7g	99.99%
Monounsaturated Fact 3.2g	0.6%
Cholesterol 27g	**10%**
Religion 27g	**84%**
Total Carbohydrate 27g	**31%**
Dietary Fibre 0g	
Total Satire 118g	3%
Includes 7g Sugar-Coated Truth	11%
Murder & Mayhem 19g	53%
Politics 9g	**9%**
Vitamin D 0mcg	
Inane Blather 729mg	57%
Iron 19.8mg	110%
Poetry 0.7mg	89%

*The % Daily Value (DV) tells you how much a sentence in a page of a book contributes to a daily literary diet. 2,000 sentences a day is used for general nutrition advice.

CPSIA information can be obtained
at www.ICGtesting.com
Printed in the USA
LVHW102121090423
743908LV00006B/184